Petals

Petals

Written by
Laurisa White Reyes

SKYROCKET PRESS
Santa Clarita, CA

Skyrocket Press
28020 Newbird Drive
Santa Clarita, CA 91350
www.SkyrocketPress.com

Cover design by Emma Michaels
Interior design by Laurisa Reyes

ISBN: 978-0-9863924-9-8

ALSO BY LAURISA WHITE REYES

The Celestine Chronicles series
Book I: The Rock of Ivanore
Book II: The Last Enchanter
Book III: The Seer of the Guilde
(Coming Spring 2017)

The Crystal Keeper series
Book I: Exile
Book II: Betrayal
Book III: Vengeance

Other Fiction
The Storytellers (2016 Spark Award winner)
Contact

Non-Fiction
The Kids' Guide to Writing Fiction
The Kids' Guide to Writing Essays (Coming Fall 2017)
Teaching Kids to Write Well: Six Secrets Every Grown-
Up Should Know

Co-authored by Raymond A. White
Evertide (Coming in Winter 2017)

For my daughter & cherished friend
Carissa

IN SIXTY SECONDS, MY MOM WILL BE DEAD.

We're driving down Telegraph Highway, the two of us, a wrapped gift box on my lap. It is rectangular, maybe fifteen inches tall, in red foil paper with a white bow on top. We were lucky to find the drug store still open on Christmas Eve.

Mom is pleased. She's humming along with the radio, which is playing a lively fifties holiday song. Her thumbs tap out the tune on the steering wheel. Her car keys sway in the ignition, jingling like bells.

Outside, the sky is dark. Through the storm, the road ahead looks like a long tunnel.

Snow is falling.

It happens so fast there is no time to react. Bright lights hurtle toward us on our side of the road. Mom's arms brace against the wheel. She thrusts her foot against the brake, but the road is slick with ice. Our car swerves.

I hear a car horn blaring. I hear the crunch of metal, the pop of glass shattering. A powerful force shoves me against the car door as everything suddenly whirls in the wrong direction. I feel pain. I scream.

And then it's over.

When I blink open my eyes, everything is white.

Snow is falling.

One

HIS WAS THE SORT OF FACE YOU COULDN'T FORGET—yet somehow, I had.

I was slumped in a chair, blocking out the airport racket with my music and a pair of ear buds, when I first spotted him slipping quarters into a vending machine. His faded gray coveralls looked completely out of place amid the crowd of holiday travelers, and I wondered if he was an airport janitor or some kind of repairman. But it was his face that sent the jolt of recognition through me. His brown skin was disfigured with long, deep scars, as though shriveled by the sun like a raisin. I knew this man, the way I'd know a song by hearing the first notes of a melody. But where had I met him? I couldn't remember.

"Are you all right, Carly?" Dad closed his Grisham novel and patted my hand. He was a handsome man, with cocoa-colored eyes and short black hair, completely at home in khaki Dockers and a polo tee.

"I'm fine," I said. But I didn't feel fine. A wave of hot prickles crawled under my skin, like they did whenever I was somewhere I didn't want to be. Dad meant well, but the truth was that I was still angry at him for guilting me into this trip.

The loudspeaker in our terminal crackled, and a woman's voice called our flight. I rolled up the magazine I hadn't read and tucked it into my jacket pocket along with my phone. Then Dad and I got in line. Once on board, I slipped my art box (my only carry-on) into the overhead compartment and shut the cover. Dad settled in near the window, so I dropped into the aisle seat, the empty spot between us my buffer zone.

The other passengers continued to board. They moved slowly, a trail of human ants doped up on Dramamine, waiting for the inevitable deep sleep of late night air travel. I tried to imagine what secret lives they might be living, like mail carrier by day, stripper by night or something.

Then *he* got on.

My stomach lurched. *Go to the back of the plane*, I thought, as if I could summon some power from deep within my psyche. I read this e-book once on mental magic, about how our thoughts influence the world around us. I tried to move a paperclip just by thinking about it. It didn't work, but that didn't stop me from trying to will Raisin Face into sitting as far from me as possible. Instead, he took the seat directly across the aisle from me.

Dad and I sat in silence while the plane taxied down the runway. As the plane nosed its way into the midnight sky, I stared out the window, mesmerized as the lights of Los Angeles spread out below me. The city from this vantage point was astoundingly beautiful, like a giant Christmas tree. My town, three hours north of Los Angeles, didn't even have a regular traffic signal. It was snowing there when we had left that afternoon. I couldn't believe I'd missed our first real snow day of the season.

After a few minutes in the air, the city lights disappeared, blocked by cloud cover. It was so dark outside I could see my face in the glass. I squinted at the reflection staring back at me, narrow bronze features framed by long, brown hair topped by a white halo.

"You can take off your hat now," Dad joked. "The sun went down hours ago."

The hat, cotton canvas with a floppy brim, had been a gift from my mom.

"I like my hat," I replied, tugging it tighter onto my head.

"Reminds me of *Gilligan's Island.* You know. That old TV show?" Dad hummed the show's theme song and took a pitiful stab at the lyrics. "A three-hour tour. A three-hour tour." He looked pleadingly at me as though expecting me to chime in.

I settled back into my seat.

"Never mind," he said, giving up.

It was well past midnight by the time the plane reached cruising altitude. The flight attendant came by, offering drinks. I accepted a plastic cup filled with Coke and ice.

"Peanuts?" she asked with a pasted-on smile. There was a swath of red lipstick on her teeth, and I wondered if I should do the polite thing and point it out to her. I curled back my lips like an orangutan, but her expression didn't change. So, I pointed to my teeth. The skin between the attendant's eyebrows creased. A possible sign of intelligence?

Dad sipped his drink. "This trip won't be so bad," he said.

"I already told you, I don't want to talk about it," I replied, and I didn't. What I wanted was to spend the next three weeks in my own house sleeping in my own bed. Why did I agree to come on this trip? I could have chained myself to the tree in our front yard in protest, but then Dad would either have cancelled the trip and spent our entire vacation making me feel guilty about it, or I would have starved to death like a neglected Rottweiler. In either case, I really didn't have much of a choice.

"I know you were mad," Dad continued, "but you're over it now, aren't you?"

No, Dad. I am not *over it.*

I scratched at my front tooth. The attendant blinked twice.

"Peanuts?" she asked again.

Dad accepted a bag. Then she turned to me, expectantly. I gave her an exaggerated grin. If she wouldn't get the hint about the lipstick, couldn't she at least wipe that mannequin-esque smile off her face? I was not normally so critical of people, but this whole situation had set me on edge.

"No thanks," I told the attendant. "Peanuts give me the runs."

That did it. Her smile morphed into a slightly unpleasant expression.

Dad choked on his drink. "Carly!"

"What?" I said as the attendant moved on to the next passenger. "I'm allergic."

"Since when?"

"Since you dragged me onto this plane and ruined my plans for winter break, that's when."

Dad opened his nuts, picked one out, and rolled it around his tongue to suck off the salt. Then he crushed it between his front teeth.

"Trust me, Carly. You'll love Guatemala," he said. He was relentless. "It won't be so bad, spending Christmas there." He poured the rest of the nuts into his mouth and chewed.

Personally, I had serious doubts about spending nearly a month in a third world country where half the people lived in mud huts.

"It's a great place," Dad continued. "Lush jungles, ancient ruins, coconuts—"

Malaria, sauna-like heat, amoebas—

"All I ask is that you give it a chance, Carly. Give *them* a chance."

Them. The so-called family I never knew. For all my seventeen years, *they* had been nothing more than pictures on the mantle. Dad rarely spoke of them, so why he chose our first Christmas since Mom had died to change the status quo was beyond me.

"Why *did* I have to come?" I asked, my frustration piquing. "I'm old enough to man the house while you're away. I can take care of myself."

"We already went over this, Carly. They want to meet you. It's important to me that they do."

"If they're so important, then why haven't you seen them in two decades?" I didn't expect an answer. I just wanted to get Dad off my back. But instead, he shrugged his shoulders and gave me an apologetic grin.

"Let's just say we had our differences," he said.

The flight attendant returned, this time offering a pillow. She was still smiling. At least the red mark on her teeth was gone.

I took the pillow and arranged it behind my neck. Dad took one as well, tucking it behind his head. I should have been glad to finally have some quiet time to myself, but curiosity got the better of me. I leaned over and whispered.

"What differences?"

"Go to sleep," said Dad.

"What differences?" I asked again.

6

"Carly, it's almost one in the morning. Even if you're not tired, I am. Let me get some sleep. Okay?"

I looked around and realized that most of the other passengers had already dozed off.

"Do you need your pills?" Dad asked.

I shook my head. "If I take them now, I'll be a zombie when we arrive."

Although, maybe Guatemala won't seem so bad if I'm in a drugged-out stupor.

"Night, Carly," said Dad. Five minutes later, he was snoring.

Across the aisle, Raisin Face had a magazine open on his lap. He licked his thumb before turning each page. I didn't realize I was staring until he turned abruptly to look at me. Our eyes locked, and in that sliver of a moment, my heart threatened to explode right out of my ribcage. I broke away from his gaze and jerked opened my own magazine, pretending to be absorbed in it.

When my heart returned to its normal rhythm, I set the magazine aside, turned on my music, and leaned back against the pillow. I closed my eyes, but thoughts kept racing through my head. I wanted to look at him again, to study his face and give my brain time to place him.

Is he watching me? I wondered. *Does he recognize me too?*

After a while, I started to relax. Oblivion was calling, but I desperately clung to consciousness, like a mountain climber gripping a rock by her fingernails while dangling above a precipice. The fall was inevitable, but I strained to hold on. It wasn't that I had trouble sleeping, but the pills kept the monsters at bay.

Finally, unable to fight it any longer, I surrendered. Falling into sleep, I struggled to recall just where I had seen that man's face before.

Two

DAD TAPPED ME ON THE SHOULDER.

"We're here."

I jerked my eyes open and sucked in a jagged breath. It took a second for me to recognize where I was, and once I did, I realized that many of the passengers had already disembarked from the plane. I recalled the man across the aisle, but most of the seats, including his, were empty. Relieved, I grabbed my art box and followed Dad off the plane.

My first impression of Guatemala as I stepped out onto the tarmac was that I had just entered Hell. Though it was barely four a.m. and the sky was still a dull ink black, the hot, humid air was stifling.

As if reading my thoughts, Dad drank in a deep lungful of it. "You'll get used to this," he said.

I adjusted my hat, tightened my grip on my art box, and headed for the terminal. I suddenly felt self-

9

conscious of the slight limp in my step, the result of my accident a year earlier — the same accident that killed my mom. At home, I'd gotten used to my off-kilter stride, but now that I was somewhere unfamiliar, I couldn't help but feel out of place.

Once we collected our luggage, a security guard ushered us through customs where an indifferent immigration official stamped our passports and waved us through to the main hall of the airport. Dozens of people scurried like insects along the corridor, and dozens more shouted greetings from an upper balcony. I scanned the crowd, first for the old man from the plane, and then for the faces of Abuela and Abuelo, my grandparents. Though there was no sign of Raisin Face, I caught a glimpse of my grandmother waving from the balcony.

"There she is," Dad said as he smiled and waved back. Then added through his teeth, "Be nice, Carly, or else."

"Or else what?"

He shot me a warning glance, but his impish grin diffused his threat.

"Okay," I said. "I'll be nice."

"Promise?"

"I promise." I gave him a playful nudge. "If I screw up, you can exile me to some distant land inhabited by jungle creatures and menacing natives. Oh, that's right. I'm already here."

At the airport exit, another security guard rummaged through my suitcase. Finally, we wove our way through the crowd and reached the exit, where Abuela waited just outside. Her gray hair was pulled back from her round face and fastened in a bun at the nape of her neck. I stood at least six inches taller than her, but she was nearly as thick around as she was tall.

"*¡Bienvenido, Antonio!*" Abuela cried, placing her hands over her trembling lips. Dad embraced her and kissed each cheek. Then he introduced me. She wrapped her arms around me and squeezed so tightly, I gasped for breath. A boa constrictor couldn't have done it better.

"*¡Ha crecido tanto! Ah,*" she said, holding me at arm's length and patting my cheeks. "*Es igualita a su mamá.*"

"What did she say?" I asked my dad.

I could tell from his expression that whatever it was made him feel uncomfortable. But he was good at hiding it. He squeezed my shoulder the way he sometimes does when he's trying to console me, the way he did when he delivered the news about Mom last year. I was barely conscious in the hospital. Took days for me to realize it wasn't a dream.

"She says," he said through a polite smile, "you look just like your mother."

I'm sure Abuela meant it as a compliment, but under the circumstances, it was anything but. Dad had spent the past year expertly avoiding the subject of my mother and the accident. No wonder he looked so apprehensive.

11

"But I don't look anything like—" I started to say, but Dad cut me off with an elbow to my ribs. So instead, I fished for a proper greeting from the few Spanish words I knew.

"*Hola*," I mumbled. It wasn't Shakespeare, but it would do.

We followed Abuela to the parking lot where a burly looking man in a baseball cap leaned against a yellow two-door sedan with so many dents and scrapes it looked like a bruised banana. As we approached, the man removed his hat and extended his hand.

"*Soy Papa Beto, su abuelo*," he said.

I took my grandfather's hand. His fingers were so thick it felt like I was shaking a baseball mitt. Despite his being built like a bulldog, Papa Beto's face was gentle and kind. After filling the trunk with Dad's luggage, he heaved my suitcase into the back seat, and then waited while Dad and I climbed in after it.

Moments later, we drove out of the parking lot and turned onto the main thoroughfare. We passed a single streetlamp, a lone beacon in the night. There, standing beneath it in the halo of light, was the man from the plane.

As we drove by, his eyes once again locked on mine. This time, I did not look away. We watched each other as the distance between us grew. Finally, Papa Beto turned the car onto the highway, and the man was gone.

Three

By the time we arrived in Reu, the town where Dad grew up, it was nearly eleven o'clock, and I was exhausted. But I tried to take in as much of the place as I could. The narrow roads were lined with squat, cinderblock buildings and trees with leaves as wide as elephant ears. The streets were bustling with people. Children, many shoeless, laughed with each other and played games like marbles and tag. Some of the women wore skirts of brightly woven cloth, while the men wore denim jeans and light cotton shirts. The two things they all had in common was that everyone was short, and everyone was brown.

Papa Beto parked the car in front of a house with bars on its windows and walls painted bright orange and aquamarine, the colors the Miami Dolphins football team. I couldn't help but chuckle.

Dad planted another elbow in my ribs, just hard enough to remind me of our agreement. "Behave yourself," he whispered, then followed Papa Beto into the house.

I stepped through a pair of metal doors and found myself in a room tiled in russet ceramic squares and furnished with a green couch and two chairs. A tarnished brass lamp stood atop a television in the corner, and several pictures adorned three walls. One was an old portrait of my family, which my dad must have sent years ago. Three faces smiled at me from the frame. I was younger then, maybe twelve or thirteen, and still had braces. I was pressed between Dad and Mom, Mom's blue eyes practically glowing in contrast to our dark ones.

I looked away before the grief rushed in.

Where a fourth wall might have been was a wide arch opening onto a veranda adjacent to an open-air garden, complete with several fruit trees, grass, and flowers in full bloom. Papa Beto escorted us across the veranda onto a cement walkway that formed the garden's perimeter. Each of six rooms faced the garden, the doors opening onto the walkway. He and Dad disappeared through one of the doors, while Abuela took my hand and led me through another. I stepped inside and set my suitcase and art box on the floor.

"Is this my room?" I asked as Abuela embraced me again. I endured her kisses, doing my best to appear grateful for the hospitality. But the truth was, I wished I was at home in my own familiar room. I hadn't wanted to come to Guatemala, but now that I was here, I supposed I should make the best of it. Abuela hugged me again, and then she left.

Once alone, I inspected the room. There wasn't much to it, really. Just a bed with a pillow and blanket, a desk with a lamp and old-fashioned clock, and a folding chair. An oil painting of a beach at sunset hung on the wall.

I pulled my phone from my pocket and looked at the time with a yawn. The bed looked comfortable, the blanket so soft. I laid down and pulled it up to my chin. My eyelids, still on California time (two hours earlier), felt like sheets of lead. They dropped closed, and I fell asleep.

We are driving down Telegraph Highway, me and Mom, a gift balanced on my lap. Slick red wrapping paper, a white plastic bow. Mom hums to the tune of the Crystals singing "Rudolph the Red-Nosed Reindeer." I hate that song. The car keys jingle, just slightly out of time with the music.

Outside, the sky is black as tar, except for the tunnel of pale beams, our headlights burning a hole through the night.

Snow is falling.

The sudden light ahead blinds me. The muscles in my arms seize up, mirroring Mom's as she yanks the steering wheel to the left, but the car does not obey. It swerves, the momentum thrusting me against the car door. I hear horrible noises crushing through my skull. Pain stabs down my leg.

I scream.

And it's over.

15

I open my eyes to the white.
Snow is falling.

A rap at the door jarred me awake. Still dazed, my breath coming in frightened snatches, I fumbled for my phone and looked at the time. I'd slept for three hours! I reminded myself to ask Dad for my pills before bedtime. I preferred drugged-out limbo to reliving the worst night of my life.

I sat up and stretched. My stomach growled painfully. I hadn't eaten since dinner last night. Voices drifted into the room from the garden. I got up and stepped outside. Papa Beto sat at a table talking to Abuela, who was in the kitchen. He smiled when he saw me.

"*¿Le gustó su cuarto?*" he asked.

"I have no idea what you're saying," I replied, though I was pretty sure he understood me as little as I understood him.

Papa Beto repeated his question and pointed.

"Oh, my room," I said. "It's fine. *Bueno*, thanks. I mean *gracias.*"

Papa Beto smiled again, seemingly satisfied with my answer. I felt the urge to retreat into my room, but the hollow pang in my belly compelled me to stay.

"Have you seen my dad? *Mi padre?*" I asked.

Papa Beto rattled off a slew of unintelligible sounds from which I understood one word: *piña*. What did pineapples have to do with my father? Frustrated and

16

hungry, I decided to try a different tack. So, I headed into the kitchen to see if Abuela would take pity and feed me.

I shoved my hands deep into the pockets of my jeans, which were beginning to feel uncomfortably warm in the humidity. I watched Abuela peel away an onion's brittle skin and mince it with a paring knife. On noticing me, she gestured to another knife on the counter beside a pile of pear-shaped tomatoes. Abuela selected one from the pile and demonstrated how she wanted it cut. Her strokes were smooth and sure, resulting in perfectly symmetrical dices. I grabbed the second knife and sliced into one of the tomatoes. The blade was sharp and cut easily through the flesh. Once I had finished, the counter was a pool of pale red juice. Without missing a beat, Abuela scooped the chopped fruit into a bowl and mopped up the liquid with a dishtowel. She mixed the onion and tomato with chopped cilantro, and carried the salsa to the table.

As if on cue, the front door to Abuela's house suddenly swung open, and a slender, middle-aged woman bounded in.

"¡Buenos Tardes! ¿Ya empezó la fiesta?"

I recognized Tía Dora from those photos on my mantle back home. She looked remarkably like Abuela, but thinner and with hair as black as oil instead of gray. She squealed the moment she saw me.

"¡Tú has de ser Carlita!" she said. After giving me an exuberant hug, she held out a basket of breads topped with colored sugar. I accepted one and bit into it. It was sweet, though a little dry.

"*Gracias*," I mumbled through a mouthful of crumbs.

"You're welcome, Mija," she replied.

A breadcrumb lodged in my windpipe, and I coughed. "Did you just say *you're welcome?*" I asked when I could breathe again.

Dora chuckled. "*Si*. I speak English. Surprised?"

"Well, actually, yes."

Dora's laugh was warm and sticky — like honey.

"I lived in New York for fifteen years," she said. "Your father never told you?"

"No, sorry. But I'm so relieved. I was afraid I wouldn't have anyone to talk to here."

Dora clucked teasingly. "Hasn't my brother been teaching you any Spanish?"

"He tries," I admitted, "but I'm not a very good student."

"Maybe Miguel can help you."

"Miguel?"

"My stepson. He's about your age. He should have been here by now, but he's late — as usual." For a moment, Dora seemed irritated by Miguel's absence, but a smile quickly replaced her annoyance. "No matter," she added cheerily. "I have plans for you, Mija. Your visit here will be a memorable one. Just leave it to your Tía."

Abuela whisked Dora off to the kitchen, and other guests began to arrive. I met Tio Raul, Dora's husband, and a horde of other aunts, uncles, cousins, and

18

neighbors — dozens of people I didn't know and names I'd never remember. Every few seconds, a new stranger would hug me and prattle on in Spanish. Though I caught a word and even a phrase now and then, I started to regret not trying harder to learn Spanish when I'd had the chance.

Dad finally showed up with a pineapple under each arm. That's what Papa Beto was probably trying to tell me, that Dad had gone to buy them. The moment he walked in, everyone swarmed around him like bees to blossoms, kissing and hugging him, patting him on the back. I stood aside to watch Dad's performance — smiling, laughing, acting like he was happy to be here.

He was convincing.

A little too convincing.

When he saw Dora, he stared at her as though he hadn't seen her in twenty years. Come to think of it, he *hadn't* seen her for twenty years, although I wasn't sure why. Back home, he had never talked much about his family, at least not until recently.

Dad set the pineapples on the table and cautiously approached his sister. After a moment's hesitation, they wrapped their arms around each other in a long embrace. When they finally let go, they both had tears in their eyes.

"Dora," was all my father managed to say.

Dora took his face in her hands and kissed him on the cheek.

"Welcome home, Tony," she whispered. "Welcome home."

Four

SEVERAL HOURS LATER, after the food was eaten and everyone had settled into chairs or on the floor for card games and conversation, the long day started to weigh on me. Though it was barely six o'clock in the evening, I had had my fill of both food and company.

"I think I'll turn in," I told my dad.

"Sure, Honey," said Dad.

He discreetly removed my prescription bottle from his pants pocket and dropped two white Seroquel tablets into my palm. "Make sure you say goodbye to everyone first."

I looked at the roomful of guests—members of a family I hardly knew existed until today.

"You remember how?" asked Dad.

Though I wasn't exactly sure if I knew the correct phrase, I was not about to give him the satisfaction of having to tell me.

"I can manage," I said. Sometimes pride could be inconvenient. I hesitated for a second, flipping through the index of appropriate phrases in my mind. Again, I wished I had been more interested in learning Spanish before. When I was young, Dad half-heartedly tried to teach me, and I even took a class in ninth grade. But not much stuck.

"*Buenas noches*, everyone!" I said, hoping I'd at least gotten close.

As I turned to leave, satisfied that I had done my duty, everyone in the room flocked around me. Each person bestowed a kiss on my cheek, and I heard "*Buenas tardes, Mija*," and "*¡Que Linda!*" over and over again. Several minutes passed before I was finally allowed to escape to the sanctuary of my room. I set the pills on the corner of the desk and laid down. The truth was that I wasn't tired after my spontaneous catnap that morning, but I didn't feel like spending the next few hours pretending to be happy when I just wanted to be alone. However, the idea of staring at the walls all afternoon was even less appealing. So instead, I picked up my art box, tucked my phone in my pocket, and tiptoed through my bedroom door.

The family was still gathered in the garden, my father the center of everyone's attention. I listened for a moment as he told a story, gesturing animatedly with his hands. From the bits and pieces I could pick out, I understood that he was sharing a tale from his childhood, something familiar to the others. They all laughed as the story ended. It was the first time in a year I had seen my father look so happy.

With everyone's attention diverted, I hurried down the corridor into the living room and slipped through the front door before anyone could spot me. I had hoped that as the sun began to set the air would cool off, but the muggy heat penetrated my skin, drawing sweat from every pore. Thankfully, there was a slight breeze, which gave a little relief and set the feathery fronds of a palm tree swaying. The sky was growing heavy with dark clouds, and the air smelled like rain.

I brushed off a spot on the street curb, sat down, and balanced the art box on my lap. The box wasn't anything fancy, just an unadorned pine rectangle with a handle and hinged lid. It had been a gift from my mother on my sixth birthday. At first, I had filled it with crayons and coloring books, but then Mom started picking up art supplies at the market.

"Look what was on sale today," she'd say, handing me a box of pastels or a plastic tray of watercolors. And sometimes she'd point out things in nature that were unusual, like a decaying tree in the forest where we camped once, or a uniquely vibrant sunset.

"You could paint that," she'd tell me, as though I wasn't just a kid scratching out stick figures and muddy smudges. She believed in me, and because she did, I believed in myself. Eventually, my stick figures became portraits, my smudges landscapes.

Resting there on my knees, I noticed, not for the first time, how shabby my box was starting to look. Mom would have called it well-loved. The truth was, however, that I hadn't opened it much during the past year. Though I still took it everywhere I went, it was hard to bring myself to create anything with Mom gone. But sitting here surrounded by the newness of everything, I felt compelled to put some of it down on paper.

I snapped back the latch and opened the lid. Inside my box lay some of the dearest things I owned: graphite pencils, a sketchpad, cakes of tempera paint, and brushes. I selected a pencil and the sketchpad and propped the lid open at a comfortable angle. Then, opening the pad to a fresh page, I brushed my palm across the white paper like greeting a long-lost friend.

What to draw?

Except for a small yellow dog investigating a soda bottle in the gutter, Abuela's street was void of life. I watched the dog for a while, sniffing, licking, trying to access the sugary remains in the bottle.

A voice called out. "*¡Osito! ¡Ven para acá!*"

The dog jerked up its head, tail wagging, and scampered toward a wiry, dark haired boy just rounding the corner. The boy wore a plain black t-shirt and a pair of Levi's. He looked about my age, seventeen, maybe eighteen.

"Hello," I called out to him, my syllables slow and distinct. "Your – dog – is – very – nice."

The boy furrowed his eyebrows. So, I tried out my limited Spanish.

"*Su perro es bueno.*"

The boy's response took me by surprise. "Osito belongs to my neighbor," he said in perfect English. Pushing a mass of wavy hair away from his face, he approached me in long, unhurried strides.

"You must be Carly from California," he said.

"And you must be my cousin, Miguel."

"Step cousins."

"Excuse me?"

"We're step cousins. My dad married your aunt. That doesn't make us related." Miguel studied me through narrowed eyelids, as if examining a science specimen. "You look different than I imagined," he said.

"How did you imagine me?"

"Younger," Miguel said with a cocky grin.

I groaned, thinking of the family portrait in Abuela's living room, the one where I'm still in braces. *The first chance I get,* I thought, *I'm going to burn it.*

Miguel stepped closer and peered over my shoulder at the blank page.

"You an artist?" he asked.

I shrugged. "Sort of, but I haven't done much lately. There are only a few sketches in here."

"Can I see?"

His request seemed a bit bold to me, and I considered saying so. I didn't generally share my work, but something about Miguel made me feel like I had to prove my ability. So, I flipped through some of the images: a snowcapped mountain, an angel, a flower. When I had finished, he asked for the pad and thumbed through the pages again.

"Not bad," he said, when he was finished. "But they could use a little color."

Heat rose to my cheeks as Miguel handed the pages back to me. I slipped the sketchpad into my box and shut the lid.

"I don't paint anymore," I said.

The expression on Miguel's face didn't change. I wondered if smug curiosity was a perpetual part of him.

"Why not?" he asked.

I shifted uncomfortably, the weight of his question pressing against me like a burden.

A drop of rain fell on my cheek.

"I think a storm's coming," I said.

"Yeah?" Miguel replied sarcastically, glancing at the sky.

I didn't like Miguel's attitude and decided that facing the horde of relatives would be better than spending another minute with him. I shut the lock on my art box and stood up. "I don't want to get caught in it. Are you coming in?"

The same wave of hair was in Miguel's face again. He shoved it back, but it fell over his eyes like a thick, black curtain. "I came to meet you," he said, "and now we've met. I'd appreciate it if you kept our rendezvous private. I'll make my excuses later."

Osito followed Miguel back around the corner. I waited until they were gone and then headed for Abuela's front door, but before I reached it, the sky suddenly ruptured in a torrent of rain.

I entered the house and crept silently back to my room. Closing the door behind me, I laid down on the bed. Unfamiliar sounds reached my ears: the voices of my father's family, birds chirping and squawking, a neighbor's radio blaring. I thought of the sounds from my own home: the crackle of logs in the wood burning stove, the laughter of my friends playing in the snow, and dogs barking. I longed to be there, back in my own home.

I had never felt so alone.

Five

AFTER A LONG, COMATOSE NIGHT, I woke up with my head in a fog.

Where am I?

I opened my eyes and found myself face to face with a pale green lizard clinging to the wall with tiny suction cup fingers. It licked one eye with its pink tongue and then scampered away.

Oh yeah, I told myself, *I'm in Hell.*

I sat up groggily and pressed my feet to the floor. Someone had draped a clean towel over the chair. I grabbed the towel and headed to the bathroom for a shower. Abuela's garden was quiet this morning, the leaves on the plants studded with dew. My dad and grandparents were still in bed. I had hoped the mornings here would provide some respite from the unrelenting heat, but that wasn't the case. Despite the early hour, I was sticky with sweat.

I reached the bathroom at the end of the corridor and switched on the light. In an instant, the floor sprang to life as half a dozen black cockroaches, each the length of a finger, scurried away in every direction. I shrieked.

Reptiles I can handle. Bugs are another matter entirely.

In three seconds flat, Dad and Abuela, still dressed in pajamas and slippers, appeared beside me.

"What is it?" asked Dad, out of breath from running.

I pointed to the critters huddled in the corners. "I am not going in there!"

Abuela seemed embarrassed, and a torrent of unfamiliar sounds cascaded from her lips, what I assumed was some sort of apology or explanation.

Dad translated. "She says she cleans, but the bugs come in for the water. They won't hurt you," he added. "Just ignore them."

"Ignore them?" I said. "But look at them! They're huge!" A roach scurried from one corner to another. I jumped back with another shriek. "What if they crawl up my leg or get in my clothes?"

Abuela removed her slippers and handed them to me.

"Take them," Dad said.

"I don't want to wear someone else's—"

Dad shot me a warning look. "Your grandmother feels bad enough as it is. Just wear the slippers."

I mumbled a *gracias* and slipped them on my feet.

Once I was alone again, I warily maneuvered around the roaches, undressed, and stepped into the shower. Another roach clung to the side of the stall. I wanted to wretch, but resisted the urge.

I turned the knob, and a cascade of water shot out of the showerhead. I waved my hand through it. Ice cold. I turned the knob farther to the right. It took several minutes before I realized that the water was not getting any warmer.

I stepped in anyway. The cold water felt surprisingly refreshing.

After my shower, I donned a white T-shirt, a pair of jeans, and my hat. I found Abuela at the breakfast table.

"¿Durmió bien?" she asked, rolling a slice of cheese in a tortilla.

Dormiste. It took a second for me locate the word in my brain.

"Si," I answered. "I slept just great."

I smiled politely, hiding my sarcasm.

Abuela handed me the tortilla.

"Thanks, but I like cereal for breakfast," I said. "Cereal. You know—Captain Crunch? Honeycomb?"

Abuela smiled and offered another tortilla, which I accepted along with a glass of juice. The tortilla was actually pretty tasty. I ate two more before Dad emerged from his bedroom wearing shorts and a t-shirt. He looked comfortable and relaxed. Like he'd come home.

"Morning," he said, planting a kiss on the top of my head. "I see you survived your shower."

He took a tortilla in his palm and rolled it like he'd done it a thousand times before. I guessed he had. No wonder he seemed so at ease. This was the home of his childhood, his family, his world. I didn't know much about his growing up years. But I did know that at eighteen, he had left Guatemala and moved to the United States, a land and culture that were not his own. He learned English. Went to school. Got a job. He met my mother when she was a librarian at the university. He studied long hours just to watch her shelve books. They were an unlikely pair. She was from a wealthy family, her father an attorney. She studied law too, wanted to change the world. But instead she married the cute Latino without a dime to his name.

But she loved him, and love conquers all, doesn't it?

After breakfast, Tía Dora came by to accompany Abuela to the market and invited me to come along. Walking into town gave me the first opportunity to see Reu up close. The town felt old; many of its many buildings needed a fresh coat of paint. But Reu seemed to lack a sense of urgency, unlike Los Angles where people were always in a hurry, day and night. Here, men with thick mustaches and straw hats reclined against the walls and conversed happily with each other. Women strolled along the roads, holding their children's hands. Other children stood on street corners selling packets of chewing gum. I stopped beside one little girl who looked no more than four or five years old. Her dark hair hung in two braids down her back.

I couldn't help but stare at her. She reminded me of myself at that age, braids and all. I recalled the boy who'd sat behind me in kindergarten, how he'd made a daily ritual of pulling my hair and calling me names. The memory was one I'd forgotten long ago, and I felt irritated that it would come back now.

The girl held out her hands, a pack of gum in one and nothing in the other. I reached into my pocket and put a quarter on her outstretched palm. By her expression, I could tell this was an unexpected windfall. Abuela and Dora had continued walking, so I hurried to catch up when suddenly, I felt someone tug at the back of my shirt.

The girl with the braids had followed me. She held out her hand, her fingers rolled into a tiny fist. At first, I thought she wanted more money, but she unrolled her fingers and there in her hand was the pack of gum. I picked up the gum and thanked her, and she scampered back to her corner.

We continued past a majestic Catholic church and the city hall to a plaza, where the market bustled with buyers and sellers. As we entered the semi-enclosed bazaar, I was immediately overcome with the pungent odor of raw meat and plucked chickens that hung from the ceiling. I covered my nose with my shirt collar to keep out the smell.

Farther in, row upon row of peddlers sold all kinds of fruits and vegetables: oranges, plantains, potatoes, yams, mangoes, and many other varieties I didn't recognize.

Abuela filled her basket and we moved on to where the tourist items were sold. Piles of hand-embroidered tablecloths reached clear to the ceiling. Earrings made from colorful beads, leather wallets, and hand-carved wooden figurines lined the shelves. But what caught my eye were the jackets. Sewn from colorful cloth, each was embroidered with intricate patterns in the most brilliant colors I had ever seen. I tried one on. The sleeves were a bit long, but it fit well along the shoulders. I took it off again and ran my fingers longingly over the scarlet and emerald bird on the back. The long, elegant tail feathers and the royal gaze of its eye were mesmerizing.

"It's a Quetzal, the national bird of Guatemala," explained Dora.

"It's beautiful," I replied.

"It is an ancient symbol of the Gods. The great kings of the past wore Quetzal feathers in their headdresses to show their connection to the divine."

"Really?"

"*Si*. In fact, there is a legend about the Quetzal. Would you like to hear it?"

"Sure," I said.

"Long ago," Dora began, "the leader of the Quiché and his wife had a son and named him Quetzal, which meant beautiful. When he grew up and became a warrior, the wiseman of the tribe gave him a feather necklace and promised him he would live forever. Sure enough, when they went to battle, the enemy's arrows could not touch him.

"But Quetzal's uncle was jealous. He had hoped to take over the tribe when his brother died, but now his nephew would become the next chief. One night, while Quetzal slept, the uncle crept into his nephew's room and stole the feather necklace. The next day while they were walking through the forest, the uncle shot Quetzal with an arrow. The arrow pierced his chest, but instead of dying, he transformed into a beautiful bird with brilliant green plumage and red feathers on his chest where his wound had been. Quetzal would indeed live forever."

Dora finished her story. "What do you think?" she asked.

The legend of Quetzal intrigued me. I studied the embroidered patch of red on the bird's chest. I knew lots of cultures and religions had myths about eternal life, but this was one of the most interesting stories I had heard.

I was about to tell Dora so, when a merchant approached me. "*Cien quetzales,*" he said.

"He wants to sell it to you," said Dora. "He asks a hundred quetzales."

"What's that in American money?"

"Oh, about fifteen dollars."

"I didn't bring that much with me today," I told her. I handed the jacket to the merchant. "*No gracias,*" I said.

The merchant started haggling with Dora. She shook her head. The merchant turned to me again, speaking urgent Spanish.

I held out my empty palms. "No money. *No tengo dinero.*"

Annoyed, the merchant gave up on us and began prodding another customer. I followed Dora to the other end of the shop where Abuela bartered for the price of a blouse. I waited for her to finish, then I followed her and Dora out of the shop.

Before leaving, however, I paused for one last glance at the Quetzal jacket, still draped over the merchant's arm. Maybe I'd come back for it in a few days, not that I needed a jacket. It was so hot, I doubted I'd wear it. But there was something about that Quetzal, like it was beckoning to me or something.

Don't be silly, I told myself. *It's just a jacket.*

I forced myself to turn away.

Six

On the way back from the market, it began to rain. Rain in Guatemala is nothing like California rain, which is more like an occasional drizzle. This was a downpour. No, it was more like the sky split open and dumped an entire sea on the city all at once.

Abuela, Dora, and I dashed through the storm toward home. By the time we got there, we were all drenched and giggling like little girls. After drying off and changing into fresh clothes, we congregated in the kitchen.

"This weather is unusual for this time of year," explained Dora, tying an apron around her waist. "It doesn't normally rain much during our summer months, which is actually winter in the states. But the news said there is a tropical storm off the coast. I hope it will clear up by Christmas." She dried the ends of her hair, still damp from the rain, with a kitchen towel.

"Why don't you take a siesta," she said. "Your grandmother and I can handle lunch."

"Are you sure?" I asked. The truth was I did feel pretty sleepy. I still hadn't adjusted to the time difference.

"Certainly," Dora replied cheerily. "I'll fetch you when we're finished. Go on now. Take a nap."

I wandered into my room and took the sketchpad from my art box. Then I laid down on my bed and turned to a drawing I had started a few months after the accident, one I hadn't shown Miguel—or anyone else for that matter—a shapeless, as yet undetermined image waiting to be chiseled from the marble of my mind. Miguel's comment from yesterday bumped around in my brain: *It needs a little color.*

I held my sketch up to the light, but its drab charcoal lines seemed anemic compared to the painted seashore that hung above my bed. It really was a beautiful painting, with a wooden pier silhouetted against the setting sun. The colors the artist had chosen were so vivid, the image seemed to radiate light. I peered at it more closely. It felt somehow familiar, as though I recognized the color scheme, the pattern of the strokes. My gaze dropped to the lower right hand corner where artists typically sign their names, but nothing was there.

I set my sketchpad aside. I stared at the painting and listened to the hypnotic sound of the rain on the corrugated tin roof. Like the beating of a drum, the rainfall created its own rhythm. I instinctively reached

37

for the corner of the desk where I would normally find my pills, but Dad hadn't given them to me yet that day. It was too early. I resisted the drowsiness that was looming, but the sound of the rain and the coolness it brought relaxed me, and my mind began to drift.

I am standing in the rain, in a vast gray emptiness of rain. The water on my skin burns, the heat consuming me. But then it grows colder.

Suddenly, I am inside my bedroom. Outside, the raindrops have changed, now white and solid. Pea-sized pellets of hail fall with determination, rattling against the doors and windows like an angry spirit struggling to get in. I look out my window. The ground is covered with white and the chill in the air foretells the coming of snow.

I creep downstairs to my living room lit only by the remains of a fire in the wood burning stove and the intermittent glow of colored Christmas lights. In the center of the room stands our Christmas tree bedecked with assorted ornaments. I gaze at the tree, and my eyes travel up to the top branch adorned by a glass angel. The twinkling lights give it life, their reflection dancing on its surface.

The angel topples from the tree. I watch as it hurtles toward the floor where it lands with a loud pop and shatters into a million tiny shards. The light still dances among the fragments of glass, and the hot embers in the wood burning stove pop.

Pop…pop…pop…

The rain popped against the roof in a sudden surge, startling me from sleep. And then it stopped.

I opened my eyes, and for a moment I didn't recognize where I was. But when I saw the painting over my bed, the panic subsided. I was in Abuela's house. I was safe.

Seven

OUR THIRD DAY IN REU WAS A SUNDAY. Dad had explained that most of his family, in fact most of the city, would be in Mass that morning. Since Dad and I were not religious, we both decided it would be a good day to sleep in. After collecting my meds from Dad last night, I had managed to chase away the monsters and find solace in oblivion. But that solace was disrupted when Tía Dora burst into my room, and the sound of her calling my name broke into my sleep like a sledgehammer.

"Carlita! Vámanos!" she said, clapping her hands together. "Wake up and dress quickly. The clouds have broken. The sun is shining. We are having lunch at the river. *Rápido!"*

I obediently dragged my body out of bed with a groan, the effects of last night's pills hanging on me like lead weights.

Dora tossed me my shoes. "Everyone's waiting, Mija. Come and join the fun!"

The clock on my desk said it was nearly noon. Mass was obviously over. Still bleary-eyed, I dressed, pulled on my hat, and stumbled outside. The scene before me was something out of a comic strip. Parked on the street in front of Abuela's house was a jeep, the old-fashioned kind you see in war movies. There wasn't anything special about it except that its chassis nearly touched the ground. This was due to the weight of five adults and three teenagers piled inside and on top of it. Dora and Abuela sat beside Papa Beto in the front seat. My dad stood on the back bumper with Tio Raul, Miguel's father. I hadn't really paid much attention the first time I'd met him, but now I noticed the strong resemblance between father and son—the same unruly hair, spirited eyes, and strong jawline. I could see why Tía Dora had married him.

On the hood of the Jeep sat Miguel and two more cousins I had met at our welcome party. They coaxed me to join them.

I gawked at the spectacle, then I climbed onto the hood beside Miguel. He wrapped his arm around my waist to keep me from falling off. I noticed how good he smelled, some kind of cologne he hadn't been wearing yesterday.

"Hold on!" he said as the jeep lurched forward with an angry squeal.

"If we were in L.A.," I shouted over the sound of the engine, "the cops would pull us over for sure!"

"Then it's a good thing we're not in L.A.!"

41

Papa Beto cautiously navigated the jeep through the bumpy cobblestone streets and then turned onto a dirt road at the edge of town. Before long, we reached a dead end. The jeep jerked to a stop and everyone clambered off. Dad and Tio Raul grabbed an ice chest, carrying it between them, and we all began hiking through some low brush. Soon, I heard the rumble of rushing water, and a few minutes later we rounded a bend and found ourselves at the bank of a river.

The sight was breathtaking. The river was maybe a hundred feet wide, but it looked pretty shallow. It flowed from the distant mountains, thick with green vegetation. The morning rain had cooled the air a little, and everything smelled fresh and clean.

Dad and Raul set the cooler on the ground while Tía Dora and Abuela spread a blanket on the ground. There was lots of food: tortillas, beans, cheese, grilled chicken, and salad. One of the cousins pulled a glass jar from the cooler. It was filled with pickled slices of carrots, cauliflower, onion, and peppers. I dipped my fork into the brine, pulled out a piece of carrot, and popped it into my mouth. Instantly, my tongue was on fire. I spat the carrot on the ground and gasped for breath.

"Water!" I cried out. "¡Agua, por favor!"

Abuela offered me a cup of *horchata*. I guzzled the sweet, milky liquid and tasted cinnamon through the burn. When that was gone, Dora passed me a bottle of orange soda. Only once the fire had subsided did I notice everyone else snickering at me.

"*¿Pica?*" asked Papa Beto, stifling a chuckle.

"Yes, it was hot!" I replied, angry and embarrassed. Dora held up the jar and pointed to the tiny green seeds floating near the bottom.

"Chiltepes," she said.

"You mean to tell me those little things are responsible for charring my mouth?"

A grin spread across Dora's face. She covered her mouth with her hand, hiding a giggle. I couldn't help but laugh too.

After lunch, Papa Beto produced a soccer ball. He, Dad, Raul, and the cousins busied themselves by kicking it up and down the riverbank while Dora and Abuela packed away the remains of the picnic.

I strolled to the river's edge and watched how the surface of the water flowed in patterned ripples. Sheets of water several inches high swept over the river's surface like miniature tidal waves. One sheet followed another, coming in bursts, as if the water were blood pulsing in an artery.

As the afternoon progressed, the heat returned. I was tempted to take a swim to cool off.

"Don't let this river fool you." Miguel stepped up beside me, joining me on the bank. "Go ahead," he said. "Touch the water."

I bent over and waved my hand through it. It was bathwater warm. Miguel pointed towards one of the mountain peaks.

"Santiaguito is a volcano," he explained. "Its lava warms the water. The river carries silt down from the mountain. My father told me that ten years ago, it flowed through a deep gorge. Today the riverbed is nearly level with the shore."

He gestured to a section of a concrete beam sticking out of the mud on the opposite bank. "That's what's left of the bridge that once spanned this river. A few more years and Rio Samalá will overrun her banks," said Miguel. "Reu will be washed away."

Just then Tía Dora appeared beside Miguel and landed a playful punch on his arm. "Don't let this scoundrel frighten you, Mija."

"I'm not frightened," I replied, but the idea of an entire city being devoured by a river was a bit unnerving. I wondered if that was true or if Miguel was just teasing me.

Dora turned to Miguel. "Why don't you take Carly to town this evening and show her around?"

Miguel visibly bristled, his carefree expression suddenly gone cold. "I'm going to the game this afternoon," he said.

"After the game, then."

"I have plans, Dora."

I felt uneasy. Miguel was friendly enough, but it was obvious he didn't want to spend the whole day with me, especially on his step mother's insistence.

"It's okay," I told Dora. "I've got some things I need to do." It was a lame attempt to free Miguel from Dora's request, but the truth was I didn't have anything I needed to do and I couldn't think of anything better to say.

Dora ignored me. She licked the tips of her fingers and smoothed back Miguel's hair. He rolled his eyes, annoyed.

"You're not going out with those boys again, are you?" Dora asked, disapprovingly.

"They're my friends," Miguel told her.

Dora took his chin in her hand. "*El que anda entre la miel, algo se le pega,*" she said firmly. "If you spend time with honey, something is bound to stick to you."

"What's that supposed to mean?"

"It means that if you hang out with bad people, you'll pick up bad habits." Dora gave Miguel a pat on the cheek. "Take Carly to the game. You can see your friends *mañana.*"

Miguel cast a resentful glance in my direction before running off to join the men in their game. I couldn't help but feel guilty about Dora demanding that he spend time with me. His reluctance was clear, but I decided it was best to stay out of it.

"Reu is a beautiful city," I said, hoping to lead the conversation down a different path. "Is it true what Miguel said about the river washing Reu away? It would be sad to see it destroyed."

"Not destroyed," said Dora, placing her arm around my shoulder. "Only changed. The river will eventually stake her claim, but what will be built in its place will be stronger and more beautiful than before."

Dora gave me a little squeeze and then walked away to join Abuela again. I gazed at the river. It seemed so peaceful and harmless. It was hard to imagine it as the destructive force Miguel claimed it was.

I thought of home, how different things had been since we lost my mom. I missed her so much I ached inside.

I picked up a rock from the shore and threw it into the water. The current swallowed it up without even a splash.

"I hate change," I said to the river. "It hurts too much."

Eight

THE AFTERNOON SUN RADIATED HEAT like coils on an electric stove. Though my hat provided some protection from its rays, sweat still trickled down the back of my neck. What I would have given for a bucket of ice.

From my perch on the bleachers, I had a full view of the soccer stadium. Below me on the field, twenty-two men chased a ball up the field. A player in a green jersey kicked it away from a player in a red jersey and started running in the opposite direction. As he neared the net, he gave the ball a swift kick. The ball shot like a bullet towards the goal, but the goalie snatched it right out of the air. He threw it back into play, and the running and kicking started all over again.

"Why is the goalie wearing yellow instead of green?" I asked between sips of Coke.

At first, Miguel ignored me, but then he answered, "He's the goalie."

"And...?"

"And the goalie always wears a different color."

From the tone of his voice, I half expected him to say *everybody knows that,* but he didn't.

A red player kicked the ball into the air, passing it to another member of his team. A green player intercepted it, ricocheting the ball off his head.

"Oooh!" I said, covering my eyes with my hands. "That's gotta hurt!"

I had seen my share of soccer games on TV. Dad never missed a World Cup championship. But I never really got into it. Miguel, however, seemed obsessed. So it was fun to mess with him a little.

When a red player kicked the ball toward the goal, the crowd in the stadium rose to their feet. Miguel's eyes were practically popping out of their sockets, his body rigid with anticipation. Another red player jumped into the air and kicked the ball over his head—right into the net.

The crowd burst into fanatic cheering. Miguel and everyone else shouted, "Gooooooooool! Gooooooool! Gooooooool!" The red team jumped around the field hugging each other and screaming.

"Is the game over?" I asked. I was anxious to get out of the sun and work the circulation back into my legs. After sitting for two hours, everything from the waist down was numb.

"Wasn't that awesome?" exclaimed Miguel, as we made our way down toward the exit.

"Sure," I responded with intentional indifference. "So, what's the final score?"

"One to zero."

Miguel hurdled the last two benches and alighted on the ground as soundlessly as a cat.

"One to zero? You mean all that screaming and cheering was for one lousy point? Haven't you ever heard of football? Or basketball? Now those are games with points, lots and lots of points."

"I never liked basketball," Miguel scoffed. "If points are so easy to come by, then what's so special about them? And football is for wusses. All those pads and helmets—"

"Those pads and helmets keep the players from getting their necks broken, like what'll happen to me if I try to jump down from here the way you did."

I laughed, but Miguel did not seem to appreciate my humor. He held out his hand and helped me down, but as soon as I was safely on the ground, he let go. I was about to make a snide comment about him not wanting to catch cooties, when I saw the real reason he wanted to be rid of me.

Three boys and a girl, all about our age, sauntered up to Miguel. The girl was pretty, with large dark eyes and glossy straight hair that fell to her waist. One of the boys was bigger than the others and with a nose that was too small for his plump face. He spoke to Miguel in Spanish. Miguel responded with a nod toward me and something that sounded like an apology. Then he turned to me.

"Carly, this is Santiago, Nick, and Tomás. We're on the same soccer team. Maria is Tomás's sister." One of the boys pulled a pack of cigarettes from the waist of his shorts and handed it around. They each took one, including Miguel. He started to tuck it between his lips, but when I let the pack pass by me, he slipped his cigarette behind his ear instead.

Tomás made a comment, and the boys laughed. The muscles in Miguel's jaw tightened. He looked angry. Maria threw me a condescending glance, and Tomás shoved Miguel with his shoulder as the group walked away. He called to Miguel over his shoulder, "*Adiós, gringo!*"

I waited until they were out of sight before speaking. For being Miguel's teammates, they didn't seem very friendly. I could see why Dora was concerned about him hanging out with them.

"They called you gringo," I said.

"It means white boy."

"I know what gringo means. But you're not..."

The sharp look from Miguel convinced me to bite my tongue.

We walked out of the stadium in silence. The crowd dissipated, and soon we were alone. A light breeze disturbed the leaves on the ground, creating a momentary cyclone on the sidewalk. When the breeze subsided, the leaves drifted lazily back to earth.

"The storm's coming back," I said, noting the dark clouds gathering overhead.

Miguel's pace quickened as though he was anxious to be rid of me. I hurried to catch up.

"So, what's so bad about being called a gringo?" I asked.

Miguel spoke without slowing, his voice tense. "My mother, my *real* mother, was from Mexico City," he said. "My father's from here, but to *them* I'm just an American, a gringo."

"But Miguel," I replied cautiously, "you *are* an American. You *were* born in New York, right?"

He stopped abruptly and turned to face me. "What would you know about it?" He shoved the hair away from his face, and for a split second, I saw anger in his eyes. But in the next moment, the anger faded.

"I'm sorry," he said. "I'm just so sick of everyone telling me what I *am,* and what I'm not. Guatemala is my home now. I just want to belong."

He started walking again, slowly this time. I followed close behind.

"Believe it or not, I sort of know how you feel," I told him. "When I was little, the kids at school made fun of me because I had dark skin and hair. They called me Indian and chocolate face. I hated it. I hated being different. I used to run home in tears, and my mom would hold me and tell me they treated me like that because they were jealous."

"Jealous of what?" asked Miguel.

"She said they were jealous of my expensive tan." I laughed at the memory.

"What about now? Do you still hate being different?"

I thought about it for a second, and then said, "I don't know."

Miguel stopped and scooped up a pile of leaves. "Chocolate face, eh? The name sort of suits you."

He threw the ball of leaves into my face. I sputtered, then quickly scraped together my own armful of leaves and flung them in Miguel's direction. As he prepared a counterattack, several drops of rain exploded on the sidewalk.

"I'd better get back to Abuela's before I drown," I said, my laugh receding to a giggle.

Miguel smiled, his earlier irritation gone. "C'mon," he said, motioning for me to follow him. "It's only rain."

We hurried toward the end of the street where a tall archway stood like a sentinel, the only opening in a high brick wall. Miguel took my hand and led me through it into a cemetery, only this wasn't like any cemetery I'd ever seen. Instead of the open sprawls of grass dotted with bronze plaques, this cemetery was a maze of tombs, colorful cement boxes six feet long and three feet wide stacked two and three high.

Miguel and I ran through the cemetery to a tiny stone chapel, where we took shelter just as buckets of rain dumped out of the sky.

"You okay?" asked Miguel.

"Hmmm? Why?" My chest heaved as I tried to catch my breath.

"You've been limping."

My stomach tightened. In all the excitement of the day, I'd nearly forgotten about my leg. "I'm fine," I told him. "It's nothing."

The rain fell harder now. It was just the two of us standing there in the entryway of the little chapel. I could hear Miguel breathing and wondered if he could hear my breath too.

"I love the smell of rain." I sat on the floor and pulled my knees to my chest. The damp air felt good against my face. "It reminds me of home," I continued, "just before a storm, when the air smells fresh and damp. And sometimes, in the morning, I don't even have to look out the window to know that it snowed during the night. The absolute stillness in the air is all I need."

I suddenly realized that Miguel was watching me. I turned away from him and pretended to study the pattern in the marble floor.

"So," he said, "Dora tells me she and your dad haven't seen each other in twenty years. That right?"

"I guess."

"So why now?"

"What do you mean?"

"I mean why come back here all of a sudden? Your dad disappears for two decades, and then *Bang!* One day he decides to come home. Why?"

Did Miguel really want to know, or was he just fishing for conversation to pass the time? It was hard to tell. But he kept looking at me intently, as though expecting an answer. Unfortunately, I didn't have one.

"I don't know," I told him.

"You don't know," repeated Miguel. "C'mon, Carly. He abandoned his family."

"*I'm* his family!"

My words came out stronger than I would have liked, and I was surprised by the sharpness in my voice. But Miguel did not react. After that, he was quiet for a while. He stopped looking at me and studied the sky instead.

When the rain finally stopped, we both stood up and walked out of the cemetery. The girl and the three boys from earlier were standing together at the corner. They waved when they saw us. Miguel waved back.

"Look," he said, retrieving the cigarette from behind his ear and sticking it in his mouth, "I was supposed to practice with them this afternoon."

"Right. Sure, I'm kinda tired anyway," I lied. I had looked forward to seeing more of Reu, but I guess the tour would have to wait.

"Can you find your way back to Abuela's?" Miguel asked. "It's just around that corner."

At least he wasn't angry anymore.

"I'll be fine," I assured him.

With that, Miguel jogged across the street to join his friends. I watched as Tomás produced a lighter and lit Miguel's cigarette, and Maria slip her arm through his. I hoped Miguel might glance back at me, give me some signal that everything was okay between us. But he was with them now, laughing, and I was forgotten.

Nine

THAT NIGHT, I SAT BESIDE THE LEMON TREE in Abuela's garden and studied the sky, shrouded in darkness. Storm clouds blocked the moon and stars from view, though I caught glimpses of them from time to time. Whenever they made a brief appearance, I craned my neck, straining to see the delicate lights I knew were up there somewhere. But then they were gone, and I was in darkness once more.

Except for the serenade of crickets, the house was quiet; the endless stream of visitors had finally stopped. The picnic at the river and the afternoon storm had left everyone tired and wanting a good night's rest. Dad and my grandparents went to bed just after sundown, but I wasn't tired at all. And I didn't mind being alone. In fact, I preferred it.

Around nine or ten, Dad slipped out of his room and headed for the kitchen. I heard him rummaging around in there, looking for a late-night snack. At home, he always got his usual—a piece of bologna wrapped in a warm tortilla. I doubted Abuela kept bologna in her fridge. Tortillas and cheese would have to do.

He spotted me on his way back to his room, a rolled tortilla in his hand. "Carly, geez, you scared me. I didn't see you there."

"Sorry, Dad," I said.

He stepped into the garden and glanced up at the sky. "Looking for stars?"

"Yep, but so far I haven't had much luck."

"Ah, well." He took a bite of tortilla, and then gave me nightly pills, which I swallowed dry. "I didn't get a chance to ask you about your afternoon with Miguel."

"It was okay, I guess," I said.

"Just okay?"

"He only took me to the game because Dora made him. He had other plans."

"In other words, he bailed on you."

"No," I replied defensively. I told Dad about the soccer game and the cemetery. "I was heading back here when his friends showed up," I said, leaving out the part about them calling him a gringo.

Dad finished his tortilla and brushed the crumbs from his hands. "I was wary about letting you go with him alone," he said, "but Dora convinced me it would be all right. Now I'm not so sure."

"I was fine," I said. "You don't have to worry."

"But I do worry." Dad's expression turned serious. "Just be careful, okay?"

His sudden unease about my safety was irritating. We were in another country. Of course, I'd be careful. But if he hadn't brought me here, there would be no reason for him to be concerned.

Dad touched my cheek and smiled wistfully. "I've got some business to take care of tomorrow. Dora's got the whole day planned for you. Hope you don't mind."

I turned my face away from him.

"You're not still mad that I brought you here, are you?" he asked.

I picked up a dead leaf and drew in the dirt with it. The truth was I *was* still mad, but what could I do about it? Throw a tantrum? Go on a hunger strike? I'd tried both those strategies weeks ago without success. So, what was the point?

"Good grief, Carly," Dad said, knowing full well what I was thinking. "How long are you going to hold that grudge against me? Just let it go, will you?"

"I don't want to be here, Dad," I told him.

"We'll go home," he said. "In two weeks, we'll go home."

"I want to be home for Christmas."

"We're having Christmas here, Carly."

"It's not the same!"

"Exactly!"

Dad nearly shouted the word. He clenched his fists, knuckles white from the strain. Suddenly, the air between us felt thick and impenetrable. He strode across the garden, yanked open his bedroom door, and did not look back as he stepped inside. Just before he closed the door behind him, he muttered the word once more, under his breath so that I wouldn't hear. But I did hear, and the sound of it left me feeling alone and empty.

Exactly.

Ten

PAPA BETO'S CAR BOUNCED ALONG THE ASPHALT, kicking up the thin layer of dust that had dried there after the storm. Tía Dora sat in front while Miguel and I sat in back. He seemed particularly sullen today. Abuela had opted to stay home, saying that she was *enferma*.

"It's only indigestion," explained Dora after tucking her mother into bed. "Too many *frijoles*, if you ask me. Your father promised to look in on her later. We, on the other hand, are going on an adventure."

I knew a little about Takalik Abaj from what Dad had told me. At home, he sometimes spoke of Guatemala's history. I recalled what he had said about the Mayans, the ancestors of the Guatemalan people. Their civilization spanned two thousand years. In the nineteenth century, scientists began exploring their vast cities of stone buried beneath mountains of dirt. According to Dad, the greatest of these cities was Tikal, famous for its colossal temples with steep, narrow stairways that reached dizzying heights.

Takalik Abaj pre-dated Tikal by two hundred years. A blend of Mayan and Olmec cultures, the people of Takalik Abaj left no monoliths of stone or dizzying temples behind. The only remaining evidence of their existence was an assortment of terraced rock foundations, which once bore structures of wood long since decayed, and a series of intricately carved stone stelas.

"It is a place of ghosts," Dad once told me, "ghosts of the ancients connecting our past to our present."

Takalik Abaj was a short drive from Reu. Once we arrived, we made our way through the gated entrance onto what appeared to be a kind of farm. After parking the car, we were greeted by our assigned guide, a slender native with straight black hair and overgrown fingernails. He introduced himself as Pedro, and then led us on foot down a path toward the ruins. Dad had described them as being spread out over several miles of coffee plantations. I had imagined nice, ordered rows of cultivated plants, like the ones in the coffee commercials on TV, but there was nothing ordered about the thick forest that loomed ahead of us.

Dora linked her arm through mine. "It's a bit of a walk," she said, "so stay close."

The four of us, Papa Beto, Dora, Miguel, and I, followed Pedro along a path through dense undergrowth and towering trees. Miguel had said nothing the entire trip and hung back as we walked. I suspected his coming along was another of Dora's ideas. Still, I wouldn't let Miguel's sullen attitude tarnish my spirits. The sights were too awe-inspiring for that. High above us, a canopy of green hid the sky from view, and the screeching howls of spider monkeys and the calls of birds resonated through the air.

My heart beat wildly. Dwarfed by nature, I felt as though this world could be prehistoric.

As we neared the end of the trail, Dora leaned close to me. "The tours are in Spanish, so I will do my best to translate what I can for you."

"Thanks," I told her, grateful for the offer. Though my meager Spanish had improved a little in the few days since I'd arrived, I could hardly keep up with Pedro's rapid conversation let alone understand it. Papa Beto, however, seemed to hit it off with him from the start. The two of them never stopped talking.

We stepped out of the jungle onto a flat grassy meadow dotted with low structures made of stone. Large sections of ruins were cordoned off, and there were dozens of numbered plaques scattered around.

Pedro's speech turned official. The tour had begun, and Dora translated softly in my ear.

"He says, 'Thank you for visiting Takalik Abaj today. You may ask what Takalik Abaj means. It is Quiché, a native dialect. It means 'standing stone,' referring to the stelas throughout the site.'"

The guide led us to the corner of a wide, flat area raised several feet above the meadow by three terraced steps of stone. These steps completely encompassed the area in a perfect square. Four houses, each the size of Abuela's, could easily have fit inside. At its base, a rough, oblong stone jutted up from the ground like a giant tooth. It stood about three feet tall and was nearly as wide. Its plaque read MONUMENTO 8.

"Long ago," explained Dora, "ancient craftsmen carved representations of deities, animals, and monarchs into stone to record the history of their people."

I responded with what I thought was an appropriate level of awe, but I couldn't help but notice Miguel's obvious disinterest. He kept tapping on his phone, shifting a few feet in one direction and then another. Finally, he shoved the phone into his pocket with an exasperated huff.

"No service?" I ventured. He just glared at me.

Pedro continued down another path through more jungle to another, even more impressive foundation several terraces higher than the first. From where I stood, I could see at least half a dozen monuments lined up along its base, like pawns on a chessboard.

We paused beside a short, squat stone marked MONUMENTO 107. The pear-shaped figure resembled an animal of some kind. Its broad face still had indentations where the eyes must have been before centuries of rain and wind eroded them away. Two arms were carved on its abdomen, its elbows bent so that the hands and fingers rested on its belly.

"Reminds me of a fat silverback gorilla I saw at the zoo once," I said, amused. "He sat on a rock like a big, hairy Buddha, his arms and hands lying across his stomach, like he'd just finished off a huge Thanksgiving feast."

I couldn't help but chuckle at the memory. Dora laughed too, but our humor had no effect on Miguel.

Pedro moved on to another monument. Dora followed, examining the stone with interest. I decided to hang back a little. Miguel was attacking his phone again.

"You don't seem to like this place much," I said.

Miguel didn't bother looking up as he replied. "I've been here before. Three times."

"Oh."

"I was supposed to meet someone but, I forgot to call to say I couldn't make it."

"And no service..."

"Right."

The way Miguel rushed through his explanation, I couldn't help but think it wasn't the entire truth. Something else seemed to be eating at him, something more than a missed date with a friend. But then, what did I know? I had met Miguel only a few days earlier. It wasn't like I'd had time to become his closest confidant or anything.

We walked several yards behind Dora, Papa Beto, and Pedro. Miguel seemed in no hurry to catch up.

"I've been meaning to ask you more about soccer," I said in an attempt at small talk. "Will there be any more games this season? I'd love to see your team play."

This only made Miguel withdrawn even more. Maybe the friend he was trying to reach was one of his teammates, or that girl I'd seen him with, Maria.

His response was terse. "We're playing on Christmas Eve."

I could tell he wished I would just go away. He didn't want to talk about soccer. He didn't want to talk about anything.

"I'm sorry Dora made you come today," I offered after a few minutes of silence. "I guess she figures, because we're so close in age—"

I let my words die on my tongue. Miguel's irritation was palpable. I was afraid if I kept talking it might only make matters worse.

"Dora means well," he said, not unkindly, "but sometimes she acts like she's my mother. She's not. She's only been married to my dad for a couple of years. My mom lives in New York. That's where I should be right now. But instead I'm here. Pretty convenient for Dora, having me around to keep you occupied."

"I see," I replied, bristling. "Well, I'm sorry my company is so burdensome. But you don't have to babysit me anymore. I can entertain myself."

I quickened my stride to move away from him.

"Wait. That's not what I meant," said Miguel, but I tuned him out and jogged ahead until I was standing beside Dora again. Why had she asked Miguel to come? Why would she force him to be with me when it was so obvious he hated me? I couldn't blame Miguel. It wasn't his fault I showed up to ruin all his plans. If I had had my way, I'd still be back in California.

We followed Pedro a little further and stopped beside an unusually large stela. Unlike the others, this one towered above us. It was flat on both sides, front and back, and its top curved evenly. Lying directly in front of it on the ground was an even larger stone in the shape of a perfect circle.

"Stela five is one of the most important finds here at Takalik Abaj," Dora said. I did my best to focus on her translation, but I was still seething from Miguel's comments. "The stela is carved with many impressive figures depicting eras of great kings and deities, though much of the surface has been eroded. Locals still come here at night to burn candles and incense."

Dora took my arm and pulled me close to her. "It looks like a giant headstone, don't you think?"

My eyes traced the stela's outline. I hadn't noticed the similarity before, but now...

A shiver ran down my spine, and I couldn't help but gasp. Standing beside the stela was a man I could have sworn wasn't there a moment before. His sudden appearance startled me, and I instantly recognized him as Raisin Face, the old man from the plane.

Why was he here? Had he known I'd be at the ruins today? But of course not. It was just a coincidence, our being here at the same time. Takalik Abaj was one of the biggest tourist attractions in this part of the country. Why wouldn't he be here? Whoever he was…

As I followed Dora and the others to the next exhibit, I watched Raisin Face from the corner of my eye. He watched me too, with dark eyes deeply set in his scarred face. Those eyes, and the sadness in them, remained fixed in my mind long after our tour was over.

Eleven

I AM LYING IN THE SNOW, my arms and legs spread out in the shape of an 'X.' I move them up and down, making a pattern in the snow. My skin feels prickly and raw. I'm not dressed right. My boots and my gloves are missing. I shiver as snowflakes begin to fall. As they do, they change from white to red, and I realize they are petals – rose petals falling from the sky.

I reach out to catch one, but when it alights on my hand, red liquid pools in my palm. The other petals fall on the snow around me, but I realize with horror that they aren't petals at all.

They're blood.

It was raining again.

The sudden drop in temperature each afternoon and the inevitable downpour that followed had the same effect on me as an overdose of my Seroquel. Every time it started to rain, I became overwhelmingly drowsy. In the week I had been in Guatemala, it had become my afternoon ritual to curl up on my bed and fall asleep to the lullaby of rain pelting the tin roof. But as certain as sleep was the certainty that I would wake up in a cold sweat, my heart pounding, my lungs gasping for air. The rain would have stopped by then, and the stillness in the air always seemed surreal.

Today was no different. I awoke with a jolt. The thrumming of my heart the only evidence of a dream already forgotten. When I had fallen asleep, I had been thinking about Raisin Face and the improbability of seeing him at the ruins. The question of who he was and how I knew him kept nagging at me. But no matter how hard I tried to remember, it was no use.

The tile floor felt cool against the bottoms of my feet. I strode to my bedroom door and flung it open as though my visions might still be lurking on the other side. But there was only the garden, carpeted in soft green grass and capped by dull gray sky.

I drew a deep breath and released it slowly, then drew another.

It was a dream, I assured myself. *Only a dream.*

I closed the door and lay back down on the bed, but a moment later, there was a knock at the door.

Dad popped his head into my room. "You all right?" he asked, concern in his voice. "You called out in your sleep."

"I'm fine now," I told him. My voice was sharper than I intended. We had pretty much avoided each other the past few days. I was still angry with him and didn't feel like making up. Besides, I was exhausted and wanted to go back to sleep, but there wasn't much point to it since the dreams were sure to return. "I'll just lie here for a while," I said. "Maybe later I'll take a walk or something."

"Today's a good day for walking," said Dad as he closed the door, leaving me alone again.

I wasn't hungry at dinner. Abuela offered me a plate of chiles rellenos, but I waved it away. I managed to down a glass of horchata before dismissing myself from the table and retreating with my art box to a far corner of the garden.

It was nearly five o'clock when I felt the presence of someone standing near me. I glanced over my shoulder and saw Miguel watching me, a remorseful look on his face.

"How long have you been there?" I asked, a little irritated by the unexpected intrusion but also grateful for the company.

"Long enough." He rocked back and forth from toe to heel as if waiting impatiently for something to happen.

"What do you want?"

"To apologize."

I intentionally did not look up from my artwork. "All right," I said.

He seemed surprised. "All right?"

"All right," I repeated. "Apologize."

His face turned red as he realized I had no intention of being polite.

He cleared his throat nervously. "I'm sorry for my behavior yesterday at the ruins. I was rude. I was pissed, but I shouldn't have taken it out on you."

"And?"

"And I actually kind of like keeping you busy."

"And?"

"And…" He looked quizzically at me, but continued. "And will you forgive me?"

I slid my pencil into the notebook's binding. But I still did not look up. "I suppose so."

Miguel laughed in mock offense. "You suppose so? Well, that's big of you."

I dared a quick glance. Miguel was smiling. I allowed myself the merest of smiles too. Then resumed drawing.

Miguel waited a minute or two, but I could tell he was getting impatient. I put my pencil down once more.

"What is it, Miguel? You're making me anxious."

"You're not going to spend the *whole* afternoon here in the garden, are you?" he asked.

"I will unless something more interesting comes along."

"It has. Here I am," Miguel announced, stretching out his arms and bowing. "I believe I still owe you a tour of Reu. But we should hurry. The fair starts tonight."

"And I should go with you because…?"

"Because I want to buy firecrackers," he exclaimed with his usual *everyone-knows-that* tone.

I thought of the stories my father had told me, how he had loved the noise and celebrations of Navidad as a boy. Though he never came right out and said so, I could tell by the wistful way he described his childhood that he missed it.

"Well, we *gringos* only burn firecrackers on the Fourth of July," I teased.

Miguel guffawed loudly. "It wouldn't be Christmas without firecrackers. Now, are you coming or not?"

It was clear that Miguel had already let bygones be bygones. So, why shouldn't I? Besides, his apology had seemed sincere enough, and the truth was, even if he didn't enjoy my company, I enjoyed his. But how could he expect me to just forget how he'd treated me?

"Listen," he said, "I really am sorry about yesterday. It wasn't about you, okay? There was something else. Just—" He pushed out an exasperated breath. "Let's go have some fun. All right?"

Looking for firecrackers at the fair did sound more exciting than my immediate plans, and Miguel seemed honestly sincere. So, I agreed to go with him. As I started putting my art supplies away, Miguel stole a glance at my sketchpad and wrinkled his nose at the fuzzy gray image on the paper.

"What is that?" he asked curiously.

I dropped my pencil into the box. "I'm not sure yet," I replied. "There's this image in my mind, but it's hard to make out. Like it's hidden in a fog or something."

"Why don't you just draw what you see? Like this tree." Miguel patted the lemon tree like it was an old friend. "It's right here in front of you. Just draw it the way you see it."

"It's not that simple." I placed the sketchpad inside my art box, closed the lid, and locked it. "There's more to a thing than the way it looks on the outside."

I realized by Miguel's confused expression that no explanation I could give would make him understand an idea that was vague even to me. I decided it was best not to try.

"You're right," I conceded. "I should draw a tree."

Twelve

WHEN MIGUEL AND I REACHED THE CENTER OF TOWN, Reu was buzzing with life. Vendors in wooden stalls lined the streets selling fresh fruit, balloons, toys, and churros. There were games, too: BB rifle shooting, Bingo, and more. The sounds of children laughing and people cheering were like a shot in the arm. I felt a sudden burst of energy, and I pulled Miguel along, wanting to take everything in.

It wasn't long before we had what we came for. Miguel paid the man for a bag of firecrackers and tucked it beneath his arm. I slipped my hand through his elbow.

"Where to now?" I asked.

Miguel led me along the street near the Catholic church, and I heard the faint notes of a familiar melody.

"I know that song!" I cried excitedly. "That's 'Jingle Bells'!"

As we hurried our pace, the music grew louder. Soon we reached the edge of a crowd gathered at the foot of the church steps. At the top stood three large marimbas, instruments resembling xylophones with wide wooden keys. Six men in bright costumes played them with mallets in their hands. The cheerful tune lifted my spirits even more. I hummed the notes until the song ended. The band started another song, "Silent Night," and a wave of homesickness washed over me. Suddenly, I didn't feel so cheerful anymore.

"Let's go," I said, pulling Miguel away from the marimba.

He smiled at me like a mischievous little boy. He left me behind and ran up the church steps, taking two and three at a time. He signaled for me to follow. It wasn't as easy for me, and I felt like every pair of eyes was watching me drag my unwilling leg up the steps.

After taking a moment to catch my breath, Miguel led me through the pair of heavy wooden doors. The music of the marimba and the crowd outside died away, swallowed by the enormous cavern of the cathedral. I gazed up at the vaulted ceiling bordered by ornate statues of saints, their faces illuminated by the dozens of candles burning below. Against one wall was a statue of Mary holding the baby Jesus. Against another wall stood a large crucifix, Jesus hanging on the cross with blood streaming from the wounds in his hands, feet, and side.

At one end of the church was a circular balcony, the choir loft. I closed my eyes and tried to imagine the priests who must have chanted hymns there centuries before I was born.

"Carly, look at this." I joined Miguel beside a narrow doorway and a flight of winding stairs leading up into the darkness.

"It's the belfry," explained Miguel. "The city looks amazing from up there."

"It's too steep," I told him, taking a nervous step back from the door. The steps to the front door were hard enough. I could just imagine my embarrassment at having to heave my stubborn leg up who knew how many rickety steps to God knew where.

"It's not that steep, really," said Miguel. "I'll help you."

He held out his hand. There was none of his usual cynicism in the way he smiled at me. I hesitated, then slid my hand into his. His skin was warm, and as he closed his fingers around mine, I felt stronger than I had in a long time.

I was ready to collapse by the time we made it to the top of the staircase, but Miguel had been right. The view was worth the climb. We stood on a wooden platform beside the large iron bell and gazed out over Reu. From one side, I could see Abuela's house, the stadium, and the cemetery. From the other, I could see all the way to the ocean. I felt Miguel standing beside me. The platform was barely wide enough for both of us, so he slipped his arm around my waist to keep me from losing my balance, just as he had that day on the jeep. I caught my breath as Miguel pulled me close against him.

"Look," he said, pointing westward. The sun was just descending below the sea's horizon.

"It's spectacular," I said, though even that word paled in comparison to the beauty. We watched the sun gradually disappear, the sky's color constantly shifting as it did. I was glad Miguel had talked me into coming.

"Miguel, can I ask you a question?"

"Sure," he replied.

"Earlier, you said it wasn't me — why you were upset at the ruins. It was more than the phone service, wasn't it?"

He didn't answer at first, but when he did, his words sounded unsure. "I had a fight with my dad, that's all," he said. "No big deal."

We stayed until the sun finished its descent, then we started ours. Going up had been a challenge, but now, with the sunlight gone and the staircase dark, I became frightened. I couldn't help it. I tried to hurry by taking two steps at a time, but I slipped, and if it weren't for Miguel's steady hold on my arm, I might have fallen.

Once we finally reached the last step, I hurried outside as quickly as I could. Pushing through the heavy church doors, I felt relieved to see light again. The fair was in full swing now with colored lights strung up everywhere, illuminating the city.

I sat down on the top step outside the church. My breathing was fast and uneven. The marimba was silent now, apparently taking a short break. Miguel sat down beside me.

"What is it?" he asked gently. "Are you okay?"

Part of me wanted to tell him that I was afraid, not just of the stairs or the darkness, but of everything. But I knew that no one, not even Miguel, could possibly understand.

Miguel reached for my hand. His fingers stroked my wrist. He whispered my name, gently coaxing me to trust him.

"Carly?"

"Last year on Christmas Eve," I began slowly, but the words were harder to say than I had expected. Silence was easier.

Finally, Miguel spoke for me. "When your mom died."

I nodded. "The accident. It shattered my femur. Took four surgeries to repair it. I spent weeks in the hospital and months after that in physical therapy. It's been — a rough year."

I tried to laugh, but it was unconvincing, even to me.

We sat there for a while longer. When Miguel stood up, I was relieved that there would be no more questions. My hand was still in his as we made our way down the steps. It had been a good day after all, but I was tired and wanted to be alone.

We reached the marketplace and began carving our way through the crowd. We were like pinballs, being jostled between revelers. Then suddenly, someone rammed right into me. The impact was hard enough to knock me off my feet. My hand broke away from Miguel's, and I crashed to the sidewalk.

Pain shot through my hip where it collided with the cement, and I was afraid I'd be trampled. But then there was a hand in front of my face. I took it, and felt my body lifted from the ground.

"Thank you," I said looking up at the man who had rescued me. His eyes met mine for just a moment before he turned away and disappeared into the crowd. I stood frozen, too in shock to move.

Suddenly, Miguel was beside me, his arms snaking around me protectively.

"Are you okay? What happened?" he asked.

"Did you see him?" I said, gripping Miguel's arm. "The man who helped me. Tell me you saw him."

I pointed into the crowd, but the man had blended into the canvas of people like a mirage vanishing in the desert.

"He's gone," I whispered.

"Are you all right, Carly?" Miguel asked, honest concern in his voice.

I searched the crowd once more, but the sea of faces blurred together. "There was a man at the ruins the other day," I told Miguel. "He kept staring at me—like he knew me."

"What man? Did you recognize him?"

"He was on the plane when I first arrived. I think I *have* seen him before, but I can't remember where."

I recalled how I had felt seeing him at the airport in Los Angeles and outside the airport in Guatemala City, how he had been standing in that halo of light. And at Takalik Abaj he had been watching me, his face void of expression.

My stomach tightened into a knot. "Miguel," I said in an anxious whisper. "I think that man has been following me."

Thirteen

"SO, WHO IS THIS GUY?"

Miguel sat down beside me on the curb across from Abuela's house. We were not alone. Families paraded by on their way home from the fair, but for the most part they paid no attention to us. The only person to take notice was a young girl who turned to look at me over her shoulder, but her mother chided her, and they hurried past.

The moisture in the air was oppressive and suffocating. Menacing clouds hovered above us, heralds of another storm.

After several moments of silence, I finally answered. "I don't know who he is."

"But you said you recognized him from the plane," said Miguel.

"He was at Takalik Abaj too." I looked at my hands. They were shaking. "What does he want with me?"

"C'mon, Carly," Miguel said doubtfully. "Hundreds of tourists come through Reu every week. You seeing him again was just a coincidence."

The first drops of rain fell. We hurriedly exchanged phone numbers, and then Miguel walked me to Abuela's door. Before we went inside, he took my chin in his hand and looked at me in a way that sent a wave of heat all through me.

"There's nothing to worry about," he said.

I wanted to look away, afraid he'd notice the flush on my face. But I couldn't. We held each other's gaze for a long moment before Miguel opened the door and we stepped inside.

The sound of something sizzling on Abuela's stove and the sweet smell of fried plantains filled my nostrils, instantly triggering the growling in my stomach. When Abuela saw us, she held out her arms and kissed us both on our cheeks. Then she led us to the kitchen. The one thing of which I was certain was that as long as I was Abuela's guest, I would never go hungry.

Just as Miguel and I finished our dinner, Dad came in through the front door carrying something that resembled a green soccer ball tucked under each arm.

"Anyone for a coconut?"

He set the coconuts on the table, and I rapped on one with my knuckles. It didn't look anything like the coconuts in the grocery stores back home, which were about the size of softballs and covered with coarse, brown hair. Dad brought one home once and announced that everyone had to try a piece. Using a hammer, he split open the hard shell, revealing the dense white pulp inside. I gnawed on a piece. It tasted like plywood.

The heavy green fruit he held up now bore no resemblance to that first coconut at all.

"You're sure that's a coconut?" I asked skeptically.

"The green part is just the husk," said Dad. He disappeared into his bedroom and returned with a machete, a long, wide blade with a handle at one end. He used the machete to hack away the husk until all that was left was the familiar hairy ball I remembered, only lighter in color. Using the tip of the machete, he punctured a hole in it and handed the coconut to me.

"Drink it."

I held it to my lips and tipped my head back. Sweet, clear juice gushed from the hole into my mouth, and I guzzled it like a parched castaway on a desert island.

Once empty, Dad took the machete and split the coconut into two halves. He handed me one half with a spoon. I dipped the spoon into the pudding-like membrane and put it in my mouth. It was sweeter than anything I had ever tasted.

Miguel took the machete and began husking the other coconut. "The coconuts you get in the states are very old," he said. "These have just been picked. They're good, but don't eat too many."

"Why?" I asked, finishing off the last bite. He and Dad cast sideways glances at each other as though sharing a secret.

"Well," said Miguel, "let's just say that if you do, you had better stay close to the bathroom for a while."

My laughter surprised even me. It felt good to laugh. I glanced up at Miguel, expecting to see a look of disapproval on his face. Instead, I saw his lips bend into a grin. I had seen him smile a few times now—on our way to the cemetery, in Abuela's garden, and the church's belfry—but this was different. The heat I felt earlier went through me again. Our eyes connected—and I smiled back.

Fourteen

THERE IS SOMETHING ABOUT SWEATING—all the time— that sort of sucks the life out of you. Reu was like a massive outdoor sauna, only saunas had one thing Reu didn't—a door through which you could escape. No matter how many cool showers I took with the roaches or that I spent sitting in front of Abuela's electric oscillating fan, I could not stop perspiring. I felt gross and sticky most of the time. Relief came only with sleeping, which I was doing more and more.

While asleep, I usually found myself back home in the mountains in the middle of winter. Snow blanketed the ground. Flurries of white flakes swirled in the air. A fire blazed in the wood-burning stove, though I never felt its heat. The Christmas tree was alive with lights. And Mom was there, smiling at me.

"What are you painting?" she'd ask me.

And I'd show her the image I was creating—a beach with black sand, a pier silhouetted against the setting sun.

"That's beautiful," she would say.

But then the dream would shift. We were driving in the car. I could hear the *chink, chink, chink* of the car keys swinging back and forth from the ignition. The air in the car was cold, frigid even. Why was it so cold inside?

I saw myself: a gift wrapped in red paper balanced on my lap, the white hat on my head, a halo of light around my mother.

I heard a loud *Pop!* as if every noise in the world was contained in that one single sound.

There were roses. Red roses.

And snow was falling…

I felt a tug on my head. I blinked blearily and realized that someone had pulled off my hat. Miguel's grinning face came into focus.

"Are you awake, sleepyhead?" he taunted, dangling my hat from his forefinger.

"Give that back!" I snapped, snatching it away.

Miguel held up his hands in surrender. "Whoa! I was just making sure you weren't dead."

I sat up and looked around, still in a post-dream stupor. I had fallen asleep on Abuela's couch, lulled into the past by the hum of the oscillating fan.

"Are you all right?" asked Miguel, honestly concerned. "I leave you alone for ten minutes and you zonk out on me. Were you having a bad dream?"

A dream? No, not a dream. Something much worse.

I suddenly felt anxious and uneasy, like I'd found myself in a world different from my own, a world where I didn't belong. I tried to stand, but I stumbled. Miguel caught my arm like he had when I'd tripped on the steps in the church, but this time I pulled away.

Miguel reacted with surprise. "Hey, I'm sorry about your hat," he said. "I didn't mean to—"

I cut him off. "It's not that."

I clutched my hat, limp and lifeless, then put it back on my head to resurrect it. I couldn't look at Miguel, not now, not while the past was still clinging to me.

"Then what?" He spoke gently and rubbed my shoulder. "You can tell me, Carly."

And for a moment, I thought maybe I could, but I had already shut him out.

"Please, Miguel," I said. "I just want to be alone."

Hurt spread across his face. He pulled his hand away. I couldn't look at him then, couldn't bear to see the disappointment in his eyes. As he turned to leave, he lingered at Abuela's door as if wanting to say something, wanting *me* to say something. Instead, he opened the door and stepped out into the rain.

Fifteen

THE REST OF THE EVENING CRAWLED BY at a sluggish pace. I watched some TV and then turned in early, claiming a headache as my excuse. I spent an hour staring at the painting over my bed, trying to see beyond the horizon, to spy the ship or the island or the storm just beyond the line of sight. After a while, I took a couple of Seroquel and fell asleep with the sound of the ocean in my brain.

Morning came too soon. I took my shower and succeeded on not stepping on any bugs. Breakfast was the usual tortillas, cheese, and black beans.

"What are the plans today?" I asked Dad, who was finishing off his sixth tortilla.

"I plan to drive out to Mazatenango to visit an old friend of mine. Want to come?"

"No, that's okay." I tried not to sound too enthusiastic about staying behind, but I had had enough of meeting new people. What I wanted was a day to myself. "I was actually thinking of sketching the cathedral," I told him, which was true.

"All right," he said. "I'll only be gone a few hours. Just remember what I said. Be careful. In fact, maybe Dora could go with you. Her house is just around the corner. Just run over there and ask her. I'm sure she'd say yes."

"Maybe I will."

He kissed me on the cheek and then left in Papa Beto's car. I waited until he had gone before I got up from the table. I would go to Dora's, but not to ask about the cathedral. The truth was I felt bad about how I had treated Miguel yesterday. He deserved an explanation, or at least an apology. I considered calling, but then thought maybe a visit would be better.

Dora's house was just where Dad had described. When I rapped on the door, Tía Dora answered, clasping her flowered robe closed with one hand.

"Mija, what are you doing here?" she asked happily.

"Sorry, Tía. Did I wake you?"

I could tell by her uncombed hair and drowsy eyes that I had, but she was too polite to say so.

"No, of course not," she said. "Come in."

I stepped over the threshold into a cozy sitting room furnished with an elegant Victorian-style sofa and a mahogany coffee table. In one corner of the room stood a baby grand piano polished to a high sheen with an arrangement of dried flowers in a vase. It was clear that Dora had brought a little New York with her to Reu.

Like Abuela's, Dora's house was small but comfortable. I could see the kitchen and other rooms down a short hall. I heard angry men's voices coming from one of them. Though they were speaking in Spanish, I recognized one voice as Miguel's.

Dora glanced down the hall, looking a little embarrassed. "You'll have to forgive us," she said. "Miguel and his father don't always get along. What can I do for you?"

I didn't want to intrude, but I couldn't just turn around and leave either. "I came to speak with Miguel," I said. "Is he available?"

I had put her in an uncomfortable situation, but she had no choice but to be polite.

"Certainly. Wait here."

Dora disappeared down the hall. A moment later, the voices quieted down. She must have told them I was there.

Miguel came in, his expression hard. He was wearing sweatpants and a t-shirt, and his hair was messy, like he'd just gotten out of bed.

"You're up early." He strode past me into the kitchen and took a cup from a cabinet.

"It's nearly eight," I replied.

"I don't get up until nine during the holidays." He opened the refrigerator, poured himself a cup of milk, and drank it. "What do you want, Carly?" he asked stiffly.

Suddenly, I wished I was anywhere but here. I should not have come. I should have stayed in bed. I decided to say what I needed to say as quickly as possible and get out.

"I guess it's my turn to say I'm sorry." I tripped over my words, but Miguel seemed unfazed by it.

"For what?" he asked.

His tone was cold, but I realized that his attention was not on me. He kept looking down the hall. Whatever he and his father had been fighting about when I arrived was really bothering him.

"For being rude yesterday," I said. "You were teasing—which you shouldn't have done—but I got angry—which *I* shouldn't have done. So, I'm sorry, okay? There, I said it."

I hastily turned to go, but then I hesitated. I had to know if he'd accept my apology. I glanced back at him, hoping for a response. Miguel just stood in the kitchen, holding the empty cup in his hands. *He won't forgive me*, I thought. *I've humiliated myself for nothing*.

"That was—" Miguel set his cup on the sink "—the most pitiful apology I've ever heard."

His eyes were fully on me now. Running his hands through his hair, he stepped out of the kitchen and moved toward me in that leisurely stride of his.

"Sorry if I seem off this morning," he said. "My dad can be an idiot sometimes. Why don't you sit down?"

He indicated the sofa. I sat, and he sat down beside me. There wasn't much room for two, and his closeness made my pulse speed up.

"I wasn't offended, by the way," he said once we were settled. "I just felt bad about upsetting you. That hat must mean a lot to you."

"My mom gave it to me."

"Really?"

"On the night she died."

"Oh. I see."

Miguel went quiet. The silence between us felt awkward.

"So, do you forgive me?" I asked hopefully.

Miguel shrugged. "What's to forgive?"

The coo-coo clock on the wall chimed eight. I wondered if Dora, or worse, Miguel's dad would walk in and see us sitting so close like this. They might come to the wrong conclusion. I had said what I came here to say. Now I had to find a tactful way to leave.

"Hard to believe it's just ten more days until Christmas," Miguel said out of the blue. "What do you want—more than anything else?"

"That's easy," I said. Casual conversation was good. Just shooting the breeze. Nothing serious or emotional here. "I want to go home."

"To California."

"You should visit me there sometime. Have you ever been?"

"I went to Disneyland once with my parents," said Miguel with a reminiscent smile. "I think I was three or four. All I remember is this giant black mouse with a big red bowtie came up to me, and I started screaming my head off. You must like living there, though, all those beaches and Hollywood and all."

"Actually, I live a few hours from there in the mountains. Ever heard of Frazier Park?"

"Nope."

"It's north of Los Angeles, three hours from Disneyland. It's nothing like what most people imagine California to be. My house is surrounded by pine trees, and it never gets above eighty degrees, even in summer."

"Does it snow?"

"Not as much as you get in New York."

Miguel made a face.

"What?" I asked. "You don't like snow?"

"Snow, traffic, crime …" he replied. "I've had my fill of all that."

"I love the snow," I said. "When I was little, my mom would bundle me up in overalls, boots, mittens. I'd stake out a flat patch of fresh snow and march around it in a giant circle. Then I'd stand back to admire the beauty of snow that had never been touched."

Miguel moved closer, which seemed odd since we were already practically smooshed against each other, but I continued talking.

"No matter how hard I tried to keep it that way, pure and untouched, I couldn't resist the temptation. I would spread out my arms and fall straight back, letting my body sink into the snow. I'd move my arms up and down, my legs in and out to make a snow angel. When I finished, I would just lay there for a long, long time, staring up at the sky."

Suddenly, I felt conspicuous, certain I had just bored Miguel to death. I turned to him and smiled apologetically. But he didn't seem bored at all. His eyes were completely focused on mine. They were not brown, as I had assumed they were, but the color of rich honey. He slid his hand over mine. My heart pounded. *What about Dora?* I wanted to shout. *What about your father?* But I didn't pull away.

"Do you miss it—your white Christmas?" Miguel asked.

My head filled with memories of the past, which wrestled with the growing agitation I was feeling.

"Things are different now," I answered. "My father wants to forget the way things used to be, before we lost Mom. I think that's why he brought me here."

"What do you miss most?"

I smiled at his question because I already knew the answer. "The Christmas tree. My dad always decorated it with hundreds of colored lights. And we had this crystal angel that would sit on top. It reflected the lights and scattered rainbows all over the room. Every Christmas I'd sneak downstairs when it was still dark, hours before my parents woke up, and sit cross-legged on the floor to watch the lights. I even did it the night before…"

The words had started flowing out of me before I even realized what I was saying, but now that they were on my tongue, they tasted bitter. I hesitated. Miguel gently squeezed my hand. I squeezed him back.

"…before the accident," I said.

Accident. That word hung in the air between us like a barrier. I wanted to break it, to take a sledgehammer and shatter it into a million pieces.

"I can't imagine how hard it's been for you, losing your mom," said Miguel. "What was she like? I mean, if she was anything like you, she must have been very special."

Miguel's question took me by surprise, not that I didn't want to answer it, but no one had asked me about my mom in nearly a year. She had somehow become taboo. People who were once her closest friends now seemed on edge around me, treating me as though I were made of glass, like if they said her name around me, I might break.

Dad was the worst. I had tried several times to talk to him about what had happened, but he usually acted like he hadn't heard me, or he'd say he was busy and we'd talk about her later—but we never did.

"She was beautiful," I began. "Though she didn't think so. When I was little, I used to wait by my window every night until I saw a shooting star. I'd make a wish that when I woke up in the morning, my eyes would be blue like hers, but it never happened."

"She probably loved having a daughter like you," said Miguel.

I thought of all the mistakes I had made as a child, silly mistakes that little kids make sometimes. As imperfect as I was, she never seemed to mind.

"Yeah," I said, "I miss her a lot."

All of a sudden, Miguel's arm was around my shoulders. Though I told myself he was just trying to comfort me, it sent a strange warmth through my whole body.

"You'll see her again someday, Carly," he said. He sounded so certain. "You believe that, don't you?"

A mess of emotions swirled inside of me, like sidewalk art in the rain. I liked feeling Miguel so close to me, but I shouldn't have liked it. It wasn't right. And all that talk about my mother was overwhelming.

"I'm not sure what I believe," I said.

"Well, I believe it." His eyes were as serious as I had ever seen them. That warm sensation went through me again. I was gazing into his eyes. When I realized what I was doing, I turned away, embarrassed.

"I've talked way too much," I said nervously. "Are you sure you didn't cast some Mayan voodoo spell on me?"

Miguel slid his arm off my shoulders and got up from the couch. I felt a huge sense of relief as he made his way back to the kitchen. He turned on the faucet and rinsed out his cup.

"I'm glad you talked to me, Carly. You shouldn't keep things bottled up, you know. Besides, I think your mom would want you to talk about her, don't you?"

He was right, of course. I'd spent too much time not talking about her.

Dora came into the room. She was dressed now in a smart-looking pantsuit and was applying her make-up in a compact mirror.

"Miguel, I hate to break this up, but I need to get your father to the airport for his business trip. Tio José and Tía Anna are coming with me. We won't be back until tonight. I've left a list of chores for you to do today."

At the mention of his father, Miguel's expression turned hard again, like when I first came in. "Guess my day has officially begun," he said, barely masking his sarcasm.

"I'd better go," I said, rising from the sofa. Miguel accompanied me to the front door.

"So, are you doing Las Posadas tonight?" he asked, holding the door open for me. His demeanor was distant again, but I understood now that it had nothing to do with me.

"What's Las Posadas?" I asked.

"Don't tell me you've never heard of Las Posadas," he said, his mood improving a little. "The Inns? It's tradition. Every night for the nine nights before Christmas everyone gathers in a procession and goes to someone's house, re-enacting Joseph and Mary's search

96

for shelter to have their baby. Then there's a big party and firecrackers and everything."

"Sounds interesting," I said.

"I'll stop by Abuela's at sundown, and we'll go together. Okay?"

As I turned to leave, Miguel's hand brushed lightly against mine, shooting firecrackers of a different kind all through me. He closed the door, and I hurried away. It wasn't until I reached Abuela's that I realized I'd forgotten all about sketching the cathedral.

Sixteen

I WAS IN FRONT OF THE TV AGAIN, watching some guy serenading a señorita from the back of a horse. Papa Beto half sat, half reclined on the sofa. His legs stuck out across the floor like broken masts, and he was snoring. Loudly.

I shifted in my folding chair, wishing Papa Beto had retired to his room before falling asleep so I could have had the sofa. I considered waking him and suggesting in a concerned sort of way that he'd be more comfortable in his own bed, but I didn't have the heart.

A fly landed on his cheek. He snorted and swatted at it, then fell back into a steady rhythmic snoring.

Dad came in from his daily trek to the market cradling a box of tomatoes and cilantro in his arms.

"He'd sleep through a hurricane," he said, jabbing his thumb at Papa Beto. "Even when I was a kid, sometimes I'd wake up crying from a nightmare. It was always Mama who came running."

We watched the movie together until it ended a few minutes later, with the señorita waving a teary farewell to Señor Sombrero as he rode off into the cactus-laden sunset. Sappy, but it could have been worse had I actually understood the dialog.

Abuela came in, wagging a finger at Dad. He chuckled through an apology, and she took the box of tomatoes and hustled back into the kitchen. Another movie began. Papa Beto continued to snore.

Dad sat on the arm of the sofa. He retrieved a yellow box of Chicklets gum from his pocket and tossed me a piece.

"So," he said, "one week down. How do you like it here so far?"

I crunched the minty white square between my molars. "I could do without the cockroaches," I said. "I prefer showering alone."

"I mean besides the cockroaches. What do you think about *la familia?*"

I arched my eyebrow and gestured toward Papa Beto, whose mouth had fallen open, amplifying his snores like a megaphone.

"Besides Sleepy here? I guess everyone's okay."

"Just okay?"

"Dora's nice. Speaking English is a definite plus."

Dad popped two squares of gum into his mouth, and then tucked the box back into his pocket. "She's promised to take us to the beach tomorrow after making tamales. How does that sound?"

"Great," I said. "Is Miguel coming?"

Dad watched the TV. "I thought you didn't like Miguel."

"What made you think that?"

"Last night. I heard you from my room. You were pretty ticked at him."

"That was a misunderstanding," I said. "He's all right. He's taking me to Las Posadas tonight."

Dad's eyes remained fixed on the TV screen, but I could tell his mind was elsewhere.

"Carly, do me a favor," he said. "Don't get too buddy buddy with that boy."

I looked at Dad. Behind him, the oscillating fan clicked and changed directions.

"Why?" I asked.

"I don't know Miguel or his father very well," Dad explained. "Dora's a good woman to have taken them on, but I think it'd be best for everyone if you kept your distance."

"But he's nice," I said, "and quite frankly, he's the only one I can really talk to here."

Dad turned from the TV to look at me. His expression was serious. "I just don't think it's a good idea for you to get involved with anyone right now."

I thought of the firecrackers, our hands touching, the looks Miguel and I had been exchanging. Had it been so obvious?

100

"It's not like he's going to sweep me off my feet and carry me away or anything," I joked. "And besides, he's family. Right?"

"Dora married his father. That doesn't make him family."

"Funny. That's just what he said."

"I mean it, Carly." Dad was more than serious now. He looked down right solemn. "I told you before to be careful here. I just—" He looked away as if he was cautiously selecting his next words. "I just don't want anything to happen to you."

I tried to act like his omen of doom wasn't a big deal, but the truth was it unnerved me. He wasn't worried about Miguel. He was worried about *me*. Did he know something about the man I'd seen on the plane? Did he sense, like I did, something wasn't right here? I considered asking him about it, but he and I had never been what you'd call communicative. Especially since Mom died. If I talked to anyone, it would be Miguel, whether Dad liked it or not.

My phone vibrated in my pocket. It was a text from Miguel letting me know he'd be there soon. I got up from my chair and switched off the TV.

"Nothing's going to happen to me," I said with a bright smile. "Now, if you don't mind, I'm going to get ready for Las Posadas."

To make my act even more convincing, I gave him a hug and then sauntered off to my room. But once I was alone with the door closed, my smile faded. There was something odd going on here in Reu. And I wanted to find out what it was.

Seventeen

DAD WAS STILL WATCHING TV when Miguel arrived just after nine. They greeted each other the way men do, with a nod and an obligatory first name.

"Uncle Tony."

"Miguel."

I doubted Miguel noticed, but I could see how my dad's expression hardened when Miguel gave me a hug at the door, even though it wasn't a real embrace or anything, just a casual one-armed squeeze between friends. When Dad looked at me, there was warning in his eyes. I responded with a telepathic *I'll be fine* and an eye roll.

After Miguel and I left Abuela's, we headed toward town where a small crowd had gathered in front of the church. Someone handed us candles and lit them with his own flame, and a solitary voice began to sing. I recognized the tune to "Silent Night, Holy Night," but in Spanish:

Noche de paz, Noche de amor
Todo duerme en derredor

A young girl, dressed all in white, stood above us on the church's top step. She wore a garland of flowers in her hair and wings sewn to her dress. This little angel made her way down the steps to the front of the crowd and continued across the square. Behind her, a man and a woman carried painted statues of Joseph and Mary. The crowd began to move. Miguel and I moved with them, following our divine herald through the streets of Reu.

The single voice soon became many voices, singing carol after carol. Miguel sang along in Spanish while I joined in in English. The night grew darker, and the candles we all carried illuminated the sky like a hundred earthbound stars.

After parading up and down several streets, we finally stopped in front of a house. Someone at the front of the procession "knocked" on drums made of turtle shells. The host opened the door and invited Joseph and Mary and their entire entourage inside.

The statues were given a place of honor in front of the window, while the party guests continued to sing and celebrate. Someone offered me a cup of punch. I accepted it gladly.

"This is amazing!" I said, sipping from my cup.

"The punch?" asked Miguel.

"No, silly. This whole night. Las Posadas. It's really fantastic."

"I'm glad you're enjoying it because it happens again and again, every night from now until Christmas Eve."

Through an open door, I saw someone hanging a piñata in the backyard.

"Do we *have* to participate every night?" I asked Miguel.

I was shouting now, to be heard above the clamor of people talking and laughing and singing.

"Not unless you want to. But you can't miss Christmas Eve," Miguel answered.

"What's special about Christmas Eve?"

"What?"

I repeated my question even louder. Miguel moved closer so that his mouth brushed up against my ear. His touch sent a shock of energy through me.

"That's when they finally bring the baby Jesus," he said.

A succession of loud popping sounds riddled the air like gunfire. Dozens of people stood out on the street lighting firecrackers. Miguel led me to a spot on the curb where we sat down to watch. I had to cover my ears with my hands to insulate them from the deafening noise.

The bright flash of the firecrackers sizzled and sparked. Smoke filled the air. The constant repetition of loud explosions combined with the noise of the party inside was more celebration than I had ever witnessed. As I sat there, hands over my ears, the smell of burnt powder in my nose, I caught a glimpse in the crowd of the little angel who had led us here. I suddenly wished, more than anything, that my mother was here to share this with me.

Miguel must have noticed the change in my demeanor, because he put his arm around me.

"You miss her, don't you?" he asked.

I nodded, my eyes still watching the angel.

A firecracker went off just behind us. I jumped and let out a scream, impulsively grabbing Miguel for safety. He laughed and held me tighter. But I wasn't laughing. The jolt of adrenalin didn't dissipate. Instead, a flash of color exploded inside my brain, alternating bursts of white and red.

An inexplicable fear gripped me. I knew it was silly, that I wasn't really in any danger here. But the noise and the crowds were getting to me. I wanted, needed, to escape. I wanted to be where I could miss my mom. But I also didn't want to spoil Miguel's fun. His arms were around me, protecting me. I wondered if he could feel my heart racing. Was it wrong to feel like that around him? We were related, after all — sort of.

I pretended to smile, to act embarrassed. I separated myself from him and tried to think of something to say.

"It's getting late," I said. "I think I'd better be getting back or my dad will have a fit."

We stood up and brushed the dirt from our pants, then started walking in the direction of Abuela's. After a couple of minutes, Miguel slipped his hand around mine.

"This doesn't bother you, does it?" he asked.

I had no idea what to say, so I didn't say anything.

The noise from the party and the firecrackers grew distant as we moved further down the street. We turned a corner and found ourselves outside the soccer stadium. I recalled how annoyed Miguel had seemed that day when Dora had practically forced me on him. A lot had changed in the days since then.

When we reached the entrance to the cemetery, we stopped. We were only a block from Abuela's now, but I wished it was a mile.

"Should we go in?" I asked. I hadn't seen enough of the place the last time we'd been here. The rain had been coming down too hard. I wanted to look around, to see if maybe I could find Dad's ancestors here. But Miguel shook his head.

"The gates are closed now," he said. "And it isn't safe at night anyway. But I'll bring you back here soon. I promise."

We stood there for a while, gazing through the bars of the gates. It was as though neither of us could think of a good reason to leave. I felt Miguel's hand around mine, like a shield. If the cemetery was dangerous, I didn't feel it.

"We should go," Miguel said.

We walked slowly, and Abuela's house appeared in front of us much too soon. There were two boys across the street lighting firecrackers. One lit the wick and they both leapt back as the string of small explosives came alive. A succession of bright stars burst out of it as it attacked the air with the sound of gunfire.

Miguel and I stood at Abuela's door, my hand still in his, but neither of us made a move to go inside. I watched the boys for a while until I realized that Miguel was looking at me intently.

"What is it?" I asked, worried. Maybe he wasn't feeling well. Maybe I'd offended him somehow.

"I can't—" he stammered, "I can't leave without—"

Then he kissed me. A quick kiss, his lips barely brushing mine, but even that brief contact sent pulses of fire shooting through every nerve in my body. He took a step back and looked at me, waiting for me to speak.

"Miguel," I said, tasting his name on my tongue. "We're cousins."

"Step-cousins," he corrected. "We're not really related, remember?"

As he slid his arms around me and pulled me close to him, I couldn't decide if I should break away and escape into the house, or just let go. Before I could make up my mind, Miguel kissed me again. This time his lips felt sure and confident, and my entire body melted against his. The fear I'd felt earlier disappeared. All I could think of was Miguel and this one moment in time—the only moment that had ever really existed.

Eighteen

WHEN I CAME INSIDE, Abuela was in the kitchen cooking, as usual. It seemed like she was always cooking, though what she could be preparing so late at night I had no idea. Papa Beto and my dad were playing cards on the veranda. They barely noticed me as I said my hellos and goodnights before heading to my room.

I was still in shock from what had just happened. I could hardly wrap my brain around it.

Miguel had kissed me.

I mean, it's not like I hadn't considered the possibility of it happening, though I hadn't outright entertained the idea. He was attractive, so what girl wouldn't feel the way I did? But the reality that it *could* happen never occurred to me — until it did.

I changed into my pajamas and stretched out on the bed. My mind relived the moment over and over again, that first tentative touch of his lips on mine, the intensity of the second, the way I dissolved into his arms as he held me.

But then I thought of Dad and what he had said to me earlier in the day. He had warned me not to get too friendly with Miguel, and I could understand why. After being separated from his family for so long, he probably didn't want to complicate things by my getting involved with his sister's stepson. Even thinking the word did sound a bit incestuous, though Miguel was right. We weren't related. Not really. But did that matter? I had just broken my dad's trust in me. I couldn't help but feel bad about that.

That settled it then. Tomorrow I would tell Miguel we could only be friends — cousins — and nothing more.

But that kiss...

I had to think about something else or I was going to drive myself crazy.

I focused on the painting of the beach. At home, if we wanted to go the beach, we had to drive two hours to reach it. We made at least one or two excursions there every summer. But as much as I liked the beach, I preferred winter in the mountains.

I looked at the ceiling and tried to imagine what home must be like now in the middle of December. The snow would be a good two feet high, powdery and light as air. The moonlight would be shining, and the snow would glisten as if someone has scattered crushed diamonds all over its surface.

I closed my eyes and tried to smell the clean, crisp air and the pine trees, but what came to me were flowers. Roses, actually. Tiny roses painted on a background of shimmery white.

When I was little, my mom used to have this porcelain teapot with rosebuds painted on it. I remembered it clearly. I remembered that I wanted to play with it, but it was special and I wasn't allowed to touch it.

Funny that I'd think of that just now.

I began to feel sleepy. The day's adventures had finally caught up to me. I could still hear the battery of firecrackers being lit outside, like cannons firing.

Pop!

A firecracker erupting...

Pop!

My mother's teapot crashing to the floor...

Pop! Pop! Pop!

No, not the teapot. The angel. The glass angel...

I reached for my pills and swallowed two. Then I put in my earbuds and turned up the music. In half an hour, the world would be forgotten, but I drifted off long before that.

The crystal angel hovers for a moment atop the tree before it finally tips, hurtling toward the floor. It lands with a loud POP! and shatters into a thousand tiny shards. Each fragment reflects the lights in the tree – green, red, yellow – blinking...blinking...

Then the scene changes. I'm at the store now.

111

"Look what I found," Mom says, plopping a white hat on my head. "Consider it an early Christmas present."

For a moment, I'm surprised she's with me. I long to tell her how much I miss her, but I am forced to act out my role from the past.

I grab the hat to take it off, but Mom stops me.

"Really," she says. "I think it suits you. Look." She turns my face to the cracked mirror on the store wall.

I take in our two reflections, as different from each other as winter is from summer. I turn away, angry. I hadn't wanted to come here tonight. I should be home waiting for my date.

Mom frowns. "Carly, what's wrong?"

But I can't articulate how I feel in any way that would make sense. When I look in that mirror, I don't see myself. I see my father. And that's not who I want to be at all.

I get up from the bench. "Are you finished yet?" I ask sharply.

"Almost," Mom replies, disappointment in her voice. "The cashier is wrapping my gift."

My past self looks at my phone. There is no way we will make it home in time. Anger surges inside me.

"Can I have the keys?" I snap. "I'm going to the car."

Mom drops the keys into my palm. I turn and head for the door. "Carly —"

Mom calls after me, but I ignore her, push through the door, and march out into the cold.

I want to tell myself to stop, that I'm making a terrible mistake, but I am powerless to intervene.

I hear my mother's voice.

"Carly!"

112

"Carly."

I was practically comatose when someone shook me gently awake. I rolled over and swatted blindly at the air.

"Leave me alone," I moaned. "Let me sleep."

Dora shook my shoulder again. "Carlita, it is time to make tamales."

"What time is it?"

"Five-thirty," she said.

"Five-thirty?!" I bellowed.

"Shhh!"

I dropped my voice to a whisper. "Five-thirty? Are you nuts? That's, like, three-thirty California time!"

Dora yanked off my blanket and pulled me to my feet. "It takes hours, Mija. We have to get started."

I groaned. My joints creaked when I stretched. "What do we have to do, shuck the corn and slaughter the pig ourselves?"

When I entered the kitchen, Abuela was already busy cutting raw pork into chunks and placing them in a pot of boiling water. Arrayed on the counter were various ingredients, including a pile of banana leaves cut into squares. Abuela must have been preparing all this late into the night.

Abuela handed me a plastic bag containing a yellow lump of masa the size of a soccer ball, which she instructed me to dump into a second pot. She added water and began to stir it, her arms straining against the long wooden paddle. I noticed how her hands were spotted and bent with arthritis, and I realized that those hands had likely never known a day without work.

Once the masa and meat were prepared, the three of us—Dora, Abuela, and I—began assembling the tamales. First, Abuela plopped a scoop of masa onto a square banana leaf. Next, Dora spooned a piece of pork and sauce on top of the masa. Then I topped it off with raisins, pimentos, a prune, and a green olive. Once assembled, Abuela folded the edges of the banana leaf so that it resembled a small green package, and then she laid the tamale into yet another pot.

Abuela wanted to show me how to fold a tamale. Her fingers guided mine as I folded over one side of a banana leaf and then another. The finished product was not as neat and tidy as hers, but she and Dora clapped their hands for my modest accomplishment.

Once the pot was filled, we set it on the stove to cook. It soon let off so much steam that the windows clouded over with condensation, and we had to retreat to the veranda to escape the humidity. We found Dad and Miguel there playing a game of chess. When I saw them, both my excitement and fear from the previous night returned. I did my best not to let them show.

"I'm bushed!" I said, dropping into a chair. "Are tamales always that much work? It's been almost five hours since we started."

Miguel glanced up from the game, his eyes sparkling as they met mine. "Wait until you taste one," he said.

"Then you'll wonder how you could ever ask such a question."

I snatched the newspaper from the table and fanned myself with it. "We made over a hundred. We can't possibly eat them all."

"It's tradition," said Dora, plugging in the oscillating fan. *Ah, relief!* "Everyone makes enough to share."

I tried to picture dozens of people trading tamales back and forth like baseball cards.

"How often does this ritual take place?" I asked. "I mean, is this a monthly event? Is there a 'Cook and Trade Tamale Day' on the Guatemalan calendar?"

"Tamales are strictly a holiday food," Dora explained. "Antonio wanted to enjoy them for several days, but we usually prepare them on Christmas Eve and then eat them at midnight."

"After all that work, I wouldn't last until midnight."

Dad, who had been too engrossed in chess to contribute to the conversation, moved his rook across the board.

"Checkmate," he said, gloating.

Miguel slapped his hand against his forehead, and then raised his arms in surrender.

"So, is anyone up for a visit to the beach?" asked Dora. "The house gets so hot when we're cooking."

"I wondering when you'd say that," replied Dad.

"What about you, Miguel?"

"I wish I could, but I've got soccer practice this morning," said Miguel, pouring the chess pieces into a cardboard box. The look on Dora's face revealed that she was less than pleased with Miguel's plans.

"You have family here," she said. Miguel avoided eye contact while he folded the chessboard, but Dora was insistent. "Forget soccer and spend the day with us."

"We've been over this before, Dora," said Miguel. "I can't miss practice or I'm off the team. You know how important this is to me."

"Your priorities are screwed up," said Dora.

"My priorities are none your business!"

"Fine," replied Dora. *"No tengo pelos en la lengua."*

Miguel paused, a perplexed expression on his face.

"You have a hairy tongue? What is that supposed to mean?"

Dora breathed out loudly, her frustration obvious. "In English, it means I tell things as I see them."

Miguel stood to leave. He looked irritated, much like the day at the river when Dora had cornered him into spending the day with me even though he hadn't wanted to.

"It's ironic, you claiming that *my* priorities are mixed up," said Miguel with restrained anger. "I'm not the one who didn't speak to my brother for twenty years."

Dora froze, her usually playful expression replaced by one of shock. My father stood up, standing like an offensive linebacker between Dora and Miguel.

"Don't speak to my sister that way."

"She doesn't have the right to hold me up to a standard that doesn't exist." Miguel looked back at Dora.

"If family is so important, then maybe you should have lived up to that standard yourselves."

Miguel turned for the door. As he did, he glanced back at me as if to say *I'm sorry, Carly.*

Once Miguel was gone, Dora excused herself and vanished into the kitchen. She seemed flustered. I felt bad that Miguel had hurt her feelings, but I also admired him for speaking up for himself. Dad didn't feel the same way, I could tell.

"That boy's insolent," he said. He stood with his back to me, his hands shoved deep into his pockets.

"He's not insolent," I replied. "He's right."

Dad turned to face me. I was a little nervous, but I continued.

"You talk about your family as if they are the most important thing in the world to you. But you didn't speak to them, didn't visit them for twenty years, Dad. Don't you think that's a bit hypocritical?"

He didn't answer. I hadn't thought he would. Instead he picked up the chess box and tucked it beneath his arm.

"We're leaving for the beach in five minutes," he said.

117

Nineteen

THE SANDS OF CHAMPERICO GLISTENED like the sheen of black pearls. At the water's edge, Dad removed his shoes and socks and rolled up his pant legs. He told me to do the same, but I preferred to sit on a soft pile of dry sand at a safe distance from the low, foamy waves.

I dug my toes deep into the sand and pulled my hat down to shield my eyes from the sun's glare. I was glad the hat was white and reflected the heat rather than absorbing it, because today there were no clouds to buffer the sun's rays. Dora and my father pranced about in the water like they were children again, splashing each other and foraging for treasures in the shallow tides.

It was clear that Dad had already forgotten about our conversation an hour earlier, but I hadn't. I was still upset about it and wished I hadn't come. He had the wrong idea about Miguel. Dad thought he was some kind of rebel, but I knew better. Something was bothering Miguel, and I was almost certain it had to do with his father. The fact that he blew up at Dora over her and my dad's twenty-year estrangement seemed to me an extension of whatever was really bugging him. I decided to make it a point to ask Miguel about it the next time I saw him.

Standing in the shallow water, Dad called to me, waving something in the air. Then he jogged up to me, dropped to his knees in the sand, and held out a flat round disc the size of his palm.

"Remember these?" he asked. I took the object and turned it over in my hand, instantly recognizing the five feather-like plumes imprinted on its surface. The sand dollar felt slick and smooth, not like the coarse, fragile things so common in the beachfront shops of California.

"It's green," I said.

"It's alive," replied Dad. "A sand dollar only becomes brittle and white after it dies." He stood up and brushed the sand from his knees. "There are lots of them along the beach, and shells. Come collect some with me."

I squinted up at him and shook my head.

"Aw, c'mon," he coaxed. "You love hunting for sea shells!"

"No, I don't."

"Sure you do." Dad squatted so that his face was level with mine. His steady, unrelenting gaze pulled at me like a magnetic force I was compelled to resist.

"Remember that one summer?" he continued. "You were, I don't know, eight or nine. You had that green bucket and a ridiculously tiny plastic shovel."

I smiled inwardly at the memory of myself endlessly digging with that shovel. Despite all my effort, my hole never seemed to grow any deeper. Rather, with each wave that passed over it, the hole magically filled with sand, and I had to begin my work all over again.

"I remember," I said.

Dad nostalgically brushed his hand against my cheek. His touch warmed me from the inside out, the way vegetable soup does going down.

"You were so insistent on filling up that bucket," he said, laughing.

"I do remember. Mom spent hours scouring the beach for every last shell."

Dad's smile vanished. He looked down at the sand. The warmth inside me suddenly cooled.

"I don't want any shells," I said.

For a moment, I wondered if Dad felt the invisible bond between us snap just then. If he did, I couldn't see it because I was watching a pair of gulls playing tug-o-war with a shred of seaweed.

"Suit yourself," Dad said, and then jogged back to join Dora again.

I stood up too, determined to find something to occupy my time. Several yards beyond the gulls was a canvas canopy. A woman wearing a wide-brimmed straw hat sat beside a card table laden with glass jars. I stood up and walked over to the table. There were a dozen or so quart jars sealed with wax. Inside each one was a flower suspended in water. The blossoms were as large as my hand, with soft velvety petals in vivid hues of orange, yellow, or pink. I leaned closer to examine them.

"Are these real?" I asked, half to myself. The woman held an open bottle of Coca-Cola in her hand. As she raised it to her mouth, her fleshy arm quivered like jello. She slurped loudly. Then, to my surprise, she spoke to me in broken yet comprehensible English.

"*Si*, flowers are real," she said. "Picked from the ocean." She held up one jar after another, turning them in her hand to show me. "Beautiful, no?"

"*Si*," I replied. "*Muy bonitas.*"

"Only five American dollar," she continued after taking another gulp of soda.

I smiled apologetically. "I didn't bring any money with me," which wasn't exactly true. I had four dollars in my pocket.

"That okay," said the woman. "This one cheap."

She held up a jar half the size of the others. The blossom inside was a deep crimson color. I gazed at it for a long time. Something about it enchanted me, beckoned to me.

"It reminds you of something," the woman said.

"Hmm?" I replied, glancing up.

"The flower. It touches you. You like it?"

"Yes," I told her, my eyes returning to the jar. Beyond it, I saw that Dad and Dora had come out of the water and were putting their shoes back on.

The woman set her soda bottle down on the table and leaned forward. Her voice was gentle, like a mother trying to soothe her child with a lullaby.

"*Su espíritu no está tranquilo.*"

"Excuse me?" The words were difficult, and I didn't understand them.

"Your spirit is troubled," she said. "Maybe the flower help you."

A slight breeze picked up, and the woman tugged on the brim of her hat to keep it from blowing away. She held out the jar with the red flower.

"Take it," she said.

"No, thank you," I said politely. But the woman grasped my hand and pushed the jar into it.

"*Regalo.* A gift," she said.

Then she picked up her soda and began slurping it again.

Back near the water, Dad and Dora were walking down the beach. I hurried to catch up, the flower jar held tightly in my hands. After thanking the woman, I had clung to it as if it was the greatest treasure to be had.

Dad, Dora, and I walked about a quarter mile to an old wooden pier that extended out over the water. It was badly decayed and looked as though it might crumble beneath us.

"This used to be a busy commercial port," Dad explained, kicking aside a piece of frayed rope with his foot. "The economy went sour because of political strife, and the shipping industry went elsewhere."

Dora jabbed him with her elbow. "We both went elsewhere too," she said. Her voice turned serious, and she added, "I was far away from home, but my heart was always in Reu. But not you, Tony. When you left, you shut the door and locked it behind you."

My father put his arm around Dora. "I went to America thinking I could be someone different than I was," he replied. "But I'm home now. At least until Christmas."

We paused at the end of the pier and gazed out toward the horizon. The afternoon sunlight glistened on the water's surface like a million tiny jewels. Below us, baby waves lapped against the wooden pilings that held up the pier. I counted several large fish swim by underneath before a sudden gust of wind nearly knocked me off my feet.

"My hat!" I cried as the wind snatched it from my head and flung it over the side of the pier. I shot my hands out in a desperate attempt to catch it, but my fingers grasped only air.

The hat drifted down until it alighted on a foamy ripple, delicate as a snowflake. At the same moment, despair dropped to the bottom of my belly like a lump of lead.

Dad ran to the rail. "Oh no, Carly," he said. "I'm so sorry."

Dora suggested we go to town to buy a new hat, but I didn't reply. I just watched as my hat floated farther and farther out to sea. Only once the fleck of white had shrunk completely out of sight did I notice the shards of glass and bruised red petals at my feet.

Twenty

5:00 PM.

I rolled away from the clock and faced the wall. Soon Abuela would be calling me to dinner, but I wasn't hungry tonight.

I hadn't eaten so much as a tortilla since breakfast. In fact, I'd done little else but sleep, though my dreams were tormented by fleeting images of flower petals floating on white sea foam. Earlier I had tried to sketch what I visualized in my mind, but nothing I drew made any sense. The gray lines just faded in and out, blurring together.

At 5:02 my bedroom door opened.

"Feeling any better?" My father sounded concerned. I punched my pillow, rearranging it beneath my head.

"Go away," I told him.

"What have you been drawing?" he asked, picking up my sketchpad.

"I don't know."

125

"You don't know, or you won't tell?" He was trying to lighten the mood, but I wouldn't have it.

"Both," I said edgily.

"Okay," he said. "I'm sorry to interrupt your creative genius, but you haven't been very cordial to me since we got back from Champerico. Don't you think it's time to stop this nonsense?"

He expected me to act as if nothing had happened, as if losing the last gift my mother had given me really didn't matter. But it did happen, and it did matter—at least to me.

"I'll buy you a new hat," he added.

"I want *my* hat."

He tried to touch me, but I recoiled from him.

"Honey, the hat is gone. There was nothing we could do."

"You could have done something if you *wanted* to."

Dad's voice seemed irritated now, exasperated. "What could I have done, Carly? What?" he demanded. "Did you want me to jump in? Risk my life for a stupid five-dollar hat?"

I bit my lower lip and tried not to cry. The last thing I wanted was to let my father see me cry. His shoulders slumped, and his voice trembled when he spoke again.

"I didn't mean that." There was a long pause. I counted the ticks of the clock. Seven ... eight ... "This isn't really about the hat, is it?"

He sat beside me on the bed, and then reached over and touched my hair the way he did sometimes when he'd think about life before the accident. I moved away from him, scooting closer to the wall. But the truth was I didn't want him to leave just now. I'd been in this room all afternoon, alone with my dreams and muddled images. I didn't want to be alone anymore.

"Dad," I asked cautiously, "why didn't you talk to your family for all those years?"

I had been thinking about what Miguel had said that morning, accusing Dora and my dad of being hypocrites because they hadn't talked to each other in so long. I wanted to understand the reason.

Dad dropped his hand heavily onto the bed. His expression changed to one of exhaustion. I had never seen him look so tired than he did at that moment.

"Is that what this is about?" he asked.

"You said you had differences."

"C'mon Carly. It was just an expression."

"I want to know what you meant by that."

He hesitated and looked away. "It's personal," he said.

"I deserve to know, Dad. You owe me that much."

He went silent, and for a moment I thought he would get up and walk out, but then finally he spoke. "I was ashamed, I guess."

"Ashamed of what?"

"That's hard to explain."

He paused uncomfortably, and I thought that would be the end of it. But then he went on.

"I'd been to the states several times, visiting my uncles in California," he said. "They lived in luxury, or so it seemed to me. I was just a boy, a boy who ran the streets of Reu with no shoes on his feet, content with almost nothing because everyone else had nothing too. But there, in the states, it was different. My uncles bought me expensive shoes. They drove nice cars and had big fancy looking houses. I came home, and suddenly *this* wasn't good enough anymore. So, eventually, I left.

"After coming to the United States, I went to school. I met your mom. We got married, had you. Life changed for me, for the better. And I liked that life, enough to leave this one behind for good."

"Then what made you change your mind?"

"After your mom died—I don't know—I guess I needed to come home. It wasn't easy, Carly. Believe me. Calling Dora, my parents, was the hardest thing I've ever done."

I listened to him and knew he wanted me to understand. He expected me to sympathize with him and tell him everything was okay. But it wasn't. Not to me.

"You said you were ashamed," I said, struggling to put my thoughts into words. "Were you ashamed of Mom? Of me?"

"No, Carly, no. I could never be ashamed of you —"

"I don't believe you."

He looked at me, stunned. But I didn't care. I continued talking.

"Were you afraid your family would think less of you because you married a white woman? Is that why you never brought us here before?"

Dad said nothing, but the look on his face told me I had struck a painful truth.

"Please go away," I said. I didn't want him next to me anymore. I didn't want to be anywhere near him. But he continued to sit there, staring at me as if I had spoken in some foreign language he didn't understand. The anger inside of me grew.

"Go away!" I shouted.

He stood up but still didn't leave.

"I hate it here!" My anger was talking now. "Why did you bring me here? I didn't want to come!"

"Because I thought it would help you," Dad said.

"Help *me*? Or were you just trying to ease your own conscience?"

Dad's expression hardened. "I came here," he said, "for *you*. This past year has been horrible for you—surgeries, doctor appointments, therapy. I had to get you out of there, Carly. You need to let go of the past."

"The way you let go of your past? Never!"

"For God sake, Carly, your mother is dead! Stop acting like you died with her."

I rolled toward the wall and wrapped my arms around my knees. My lungs shook as I struggled not to cry.

"If I were you," Dad said, "I'd stop wallowing in self-pity and come eat some dinner."

"You're not me!" I screamed.

He said nothing more as he left and closed the door behind him. I picked up my bottle of pills and chucked them at the door. The lid popped off and tablets burst across the room.

"You're nothing like me!"

Twenty-One

AFTER THE BLOWOUT WITH MY DAD, I had to get away. I texted Miguel and suggested we meet up. He agreed.

The cemetery that afternoon was cool and damp. Miguel hadn't arrived yet, so I found a quiet corner and leaned against the moss-covered wall. A procession of mourners dressed in black followed a simple wooden casket born on the shoulders of six men. The women wept and dabbed their eyes with handkerchiefs. The men gazed solemnly forward. They carried the casket to an empty concrete tomb at the far side of the cemetery and slid it inside.

I watched from a respectful distance. The scene seemed so familiar. I didn't want to remember, but when I closed my eyes the images came against my will. After a while, I stopped fighting and let them come.

It was dusk.

White snow covers everything like a thick, woolen blanket. The day is bathed in shadow — crests of gray marble headstones peeking out from the snow, the women's black dresses, the white carnations adorning my mother's casket. The only color are the roses — red roses that friends and acquaintances toss into the open grave, their final good-byes.

When it is my turn, my father pushes my wheelchair to the edge of the grave. I throw my flower in among the others. The buds on the casket below are dotted with flakes of snow. I look around at the backs of the people who called themselves her friends. As they drift away, one by one, I remain beside the hole in the earth that will become my mother's tomb.

I am solitary.

But I am not alone.

A touch on my shoulder startled me, hurling me back to the present. I opened my eyes and found Miguel grinning at me.

"I know flamingos sleep standing up, but you?" he said, laughing.

"I wasn't sleeping," I replied, surprised but happy to see him. "Just thinking."

"About what?"

I shook my head and rubbed my arms with my hands. I felt cold despite Reu's permeating heat. "Nothing really," I said. "Just a memory."

Miguel sat down on the nearest tomb and patted the space next to him. I brushed off the dirt and sat down. Nearby, a priest sprinkled holy water on the new grave and began to pray.

"Hey, I wanted to show you something." Miguel held a brown paper bundle in his hands. He unwrapped it, revealing a set of hand-carved wooden figurines. "It's a nativity," he explained, arranging the pieces on the cement. "See? Here are the shepherds and wise men, some animals, Mary, Joseph, and Jesus."

I picked up a kneeling donkey. The carving was crude and simple, but it had charm.

"I thought you might like it—*por Navidad*. The tourists love them."

A gift. Miguel had given me a gift. I thanked him, and he helped me wrap the figures back in the paper. I thought about what I had planned to say to him, about being cousins and nothing more.

"You know we're leaving the day after Christmas," I said. "Just a few more days and it's *hasta la vista*."

"You're glad to be going home, then?" Miguel asked.
"I am."

"Glad to be getting away from here?"

His words stung. It was true that I hadn't wanted to come here, but now things were…different.

"If you're wondering if I'll miss you, Miguel, I will. But I promise to write." I bumped against him playfully, but his expression was serious.

"That's not what I meant." His mood started to shift.
"What did you mean?"

The priest officiating the funeral crossed himself and droned a prayer in Spanish.

"You think you don't belong here," said Miguel. "You want to go back to California, only you don't belong there either. Not really."

"You're not making any sense," I said.

"You're straddling the river, Carly, standing with one foot on each bank. You and I have that in common. But my situation is not my choice. You, on the other hand, can't make up your mind which side you're on. You know what happens to people who straddle the river too long, don't you?"

I could guess the answer, but I waited for him to tell me.

"You fall in."

The funeral ended and the mourners slowly began to dissipate. Miguel's words sank deep into my mind. What did he mean I was straddling the river? And what exactly did we have in common?

"Miguel, the other morning when I came to your house, what were you and your dad arguing about?"

A dark shadow seemed to fall across Miguel's face. His jaw clenched. He had the same reaction whenever he talked about his dad.

I reached for his hand, letting him know that he could talk to me if he wanted to. He could trust me. But he said nothing. I thought of the times I had opened up to him. It didn't seem fair he wouldn't do the same for me, but I didn't want to push the matter. Whatever was bothering him was his business, not mine.

We continued to observe the last of the funeral goers as they left the cemetery until only a man and a child remained. The pair stood beside the grave, heads bowed, paying their last respects to a wife and mother. Once their private moment of bereavement had ended, the man took the child by the hand, and together they walked toward the archway leading to the street. As they passed by us, the man lifted his eyes to mine.

The air in my lungs froze like ice.

The man's face was brown and scarred. His dark eyes bore the same sadness as when I had seen him each time before: on the plane, at the ruins, outside the church.

"Carly, what's wrong?" asked Miguel, grasping my elbow. I hadn't realized how off balance I felt. "You're trembling."

"I'm fine," I answered.

"Are you sure? You look frightened."

I shook my head and tried to smile.

"It's nothing," I reassured him, but I did feel frightened. Terribly frightened.

Twenty-Two

THE AIR SMELLED DAMP from the afternoon rain, which had stopped only moments earlier. Droplets of water clung to the leaves of Abuela's lemon tree, shimmering rhinestones on a fabric of green.

Miguel and I sat across from each other at the little table on Abuela's veranda. We had watched the rain fall without speaking, but now that the rain had stopped, the void in my mind began filling with questions.

"Do you believe in ghosts, Miguel?"

Miguel contemplated my question before answering. "There's a story here in Reu of a woman who committed suicide, a woman in white who haunts the cemetery at night. My father told me he saw her once. I guess I believe him."

"So, you think it's possible? To see ghosts, I mean."

Miguel shrugged. "Maybe," he said.

His words, while uncertain, sent shivers across my back. Did I believe that Raisin Face was a ghost? No. He looked as real, as solid as Miguel did sitting in front of me now.

"What's wrong, Carly?" asked Miguel tenderly. "Something's been troubling you ever since you came here. Tell me what it is."

How ironic, I thought. I had been concerned that something was bothering Miguel while all along he had been worried about me.

"I guess I just miss my mom," I said.

I waited for a reaction, the usual discomfort in people's faces when death is mentioned. The look that says they wish they hadn't asked, that they wanted to get away as fast as possible. But that look didn't come.

Miguel said nothing. His silence was starting to make me feel uncomfortable. I got up from the table. Suddenly, I was the one who wanted to get away.

"I'm sorry," I said, my old sarcasm coming back. "I forgot I'm not supposed to talk about it. I'm supposed to get on with my life and act like nothing happened."

"I didn't say that," Miguel replied. He reached for my hand, but I pulled away.

"No, but that's what you and everybody else thinks." I plucked a leaf from the lemon tree, ran my thumb across its waxy surface. "For a long time after the accident, people said they were sorry, and if we needed anything to call them. But they didn't mean it, not really, and after a while they stopped saying it. Everyone started acting normal again, and they expected me to act normal too. But how can I, Miguel? Tell me how I'm supposed to act normal when the only person who ever really loved me is gone?"

I crushed the leaf in my fist and let it fall. I didn't know what came over me at that moment. It was as though all the hurt and anger I'd been bottling up inside me all year just exploded. I fought back tears. I didn't want to cry, not in front of Miguel. But when I looked at him, I didn't see the shock or embarrassment I'd expected. Instead I saw something else, something that calmed me down and made me feel understood.

"I'm sorry," I said again, self-conscious of my sudden outburst. "I didn't mean to... I mean, I shouldn't have said anything."

"It's okay," said Miguel. "It must have been terrible for you, losing your mom like that. I can't imagine how much you must miss her."

Then I lost it. The tears just fell, torrents of them streaming down my face. And then when Miguel stood up and pulled me into him, I started to sob. And the funny thing was I wasn't embarrassed anymore.

Miguel held me a long time until my crying subsided. When I finally pulled myself together, he dried my eyes with the hem of his t-shirt.

"You know the worst thing?" I asked once I could speak clearly again. "No one talks about her. Not even my dad. It's like she never existed at all."

"I'm sure your dad misses her too."

"You don't understand. He blames me, for some reason. I mean he doesn't say it, but I can see it in his eyes."

"Why would he blame you? He loves you, Carly. The problem is that you're both suffering alone. You need to talk about her, about what happened."

"What's the point? She's not coming back, Miguel. Maybe everyone's right. I'm never going to see her again so I should just get on with my life and let her go."

"Do you really believe that, Carly?"

"No, I don't."

"Neither do I."

I sat at the table again and shuffled the deck of cards that was always there, just to keep my hands busy. I straightened the deck and set it aside.

"What *do* you believe?" I asked, looking up at Miguel.

He brushed his hair from his face and then slipped his hands into his pockets. "I believe that life doesn't end at death. We didn't just pop into existence the moment we were born, and we don't just pop out of it when we die. I think everyone has a soul that keeps on living."

I thought of Raisin Face, the hollowness in his eyes. Was he a ghost? Some former being that had come back to haunt me? Was this what Miguel meant by a soul who keeps on living? But if he was haunting me, then why couldn't I remember him? Each time I saw him, I was pricked with the sense that I knew him, or at least recognized him, but the details were beyond my grasp.

"Do you remember the man from the fair?"

139

"The one you said was following you?"

"I saw him again."

Miguel seemed suddenly alarmed. "Where? When?"

"At the cemetery, earlier today. He was there at the funeral with the mourners. There a little girl with him."

Now Miguel looked confused. "I did see a man and a girl," he said. "It was Don Diego, the pharmacist. His wife died a few days ago. It was her funeral."

I sat up. "You know him?"

"Yes. He and my father are old friends, only…" Miguel hesitated.

"What is it?" I asked.

"He couldn't be the man you described to me, the one with the scarred face. He doesn't look like that at all. And you said you first saw him in Los Angeles, in the airport." Miguel shook his head. "As far as I know, Don Diego has never been to the states. And last week he was with his wife in the hospital."

"What are you saying?"

"I'm saying that maybe you made a mistake, Carly. Maybe you thought you saw the man, but your mind was playing tricks on you or something."

"I know what I saw." I was beginning to feel irritated. "I wasn't imagining things. I'm not crazy."

"That's not what I meant."

"What about the other times? Did I imagine him then too?" My voice was sharper than I had intended.

"No need to get defensive," said Miguel. "Listen, you probably did see him before, I mean before coming to Reu. Then maybe something here triggered your memory of him. It's happened to other people, seeing faces from the past."

How dare he? I had just opened a vein and spilled my deepest thoughts to him. I trusted him and he didn't even believe me. But why should he? He couldn't even be honest with me about a stupid fight with his father.

Miguel picked up the card deck and began distributing them between us. "You should just forget about it, okay? Why don't we play Slap Jack?"

He was trying to get my mind off things, but it wasn't going to work. I wanted to tell him to forget everything I had said, or better yet to leave me alone. I didn't need his help. I could manage Raisin Face on my own. But then I thought of the nativity set he'd bought for me and Las Posadas and the belfry at the church. It wasn't his fault my story sounded far-fetched. He was trying to help in his own way.

I watched my pile of cards grow, cards tossed haphazardly on top of each other. I was beginning to feel like that—chaotic, confused. I had seen Raisin Face clear as anything. His being at the cemetery could not have been a coincidence. Not again. So why *was* he there? Who was he?

Miguel guided his cards into a tidy stack. "Ready?"

I nodded. But was I ready? Ready to face this remnant from my past that I had forgotten? I lifted my first card and held it inches over the table.

"Ready," I said.

Twenty-Three

THAT NIGHT, I DID NOT TAKE MY PILLS. I had hidden from my demons long enough. If Dad was so intent on my forgetting, then maybe it was time to remember. I was tired of hunting for answers in my brain only to come up empty, or worse, with murky half-memories. I wanted to know who Raisin Face was, and I suspected the truth was just waiting to be resurrected. But for that to happen, my mind needed to be clear.

I set up Miguel's nativity scene on my desk and studied the figurines until I fell asleep. I had hoped tonight would expose some long-hidden truth, but the dream that came to me was the same as always: bits and pieces from the accident and my mother's funeral. I woke up feeling disappointed.

The next day was Sunday. I had been here for ten days already, and in just five more, I would be going home.

At eight-thirty, when Miguel and Dora came for my grandparents to take them to church, I was ready for them.

"I'm coming with you," I said. I wore a skirt I had picked up in the market earlier in the week, and though I felt a little out of place with my sneakers and T-shirt, it was as religious as I could get under the circumstances.

Abuela grinned widely when she saw me and patted my cheeks. But Dora looked worried.

"Maybe this isn't such a good idea," she said. "Your father would disapprove."

"My father is snoring in his bed," I replied. "He won't even miss me."

Dora glanced at Miguel who just shrugged, but I caught a hint of a smile beneath his disinterested expression.

"Oh, all right," said Dora hastily, "but we'd better go or we'll miss mass."

The Church, which had been empty the first time I entered, was now teeming with life. More than a hundred men, women, and children filed up the steps and through the doors, open wide to receive them. Abuela, Miguel, Tía Dora, and I joined the throng of worshippers and were soon ushered onto a bench near the rear of the chapel.

"You don't have to kneel or say the prayers," whispered Dora, grasping her rosary and pressing it to her lips. I glanced at Miguel, who sat on the other side of me. He winked playfully before closing his eyes in what appeared to be a silent prayer.

The chapel filled quickly, and the low hum of whispers sounded almost otherworldly. Then, suddenly, the voices ceased. A priest wearing a white and gold robe stood at the front of the room, his hands raised just above his head.

The service was unlike anything I had witnessed before—the priest speaking words I didn't understand, the congregation answering back, standing, kneeling, praying. So that I wouldn't seem too out of place, I stood when everyone stood and knelt when everyone knelt. At one point, I caught a glimpse of Miguel watching me from the corner of his eye, his lips barely turned into a grin.

When the priest called the congregation forward for communion, I remained in my seat. Miguel, Dora, and Abuela all got in line with the others. Sitting there alone, I allowed my eyes to roam the spacious cathedral, as I had that first time with Miguel. There was that statue again, of Mary and baby Jesus, and the huge crucifix with the dying Christ. I shivered even though I was far from cold.

I turned away from the images and studied the stained-glass windows instead. The forlorn faces of saints and apostles gazed back. I let my eyes travel to the last window near the front of the cathedral. It was different than the others, and I hadn't noticed it before. While the other windows had darker hues, this one was bright, with mostly yellows and whites. It was of a man dressed in white robes standing beside an open cave. His pale skin glowed. A golden crown was on his head. Unlike the statue, this Christ's face seemed at peace, almost smiling. I noticed that there were marks in his upturned palms, wounds of his crucifixion, yet he was very much alive in this picture.

After the service, my mind reflected on that image of Jesus. I thought of Miguel's words too, that everyone had a soul that kept on living. I was beginning to believe it.

"Dad? Dad, are you here?"

I poked my head through Abuela's front door and waited for an answer. When none came, I ventured into the house followed by Miguel who had offered to walk me home so that Dora and my grandparents could stay after church and mingle with their friends. My father's bedroom door was open. I called for him again. Still no reply.

"I guess he went out," I said.

Miguel and I headed for the garden.

"I'm glad you came today," said Miguel, sitting beside me on the ground next to the lemon tree. "What did you think?"

"I liked it," I said. "I expected it to be all weird and cultish, but instead mass was beautiful. Thank you for taking me."

"Any time."

Miguel's hand slid comfortably over mine, our fingers interlacing. Holding his hand was beginning to feel natural.

"Miguel, can I tell you something?" I asked.

"Sure."

"I didn't expect anything like this."

"This?"

I squeezed his hand. "*This*. The truth is, Guatemala was the last place I wanted to be for Christmas. My dad pretty much threatened me into coming. But now, I'm glad he did."

Miguel laughed. Then he laid back on the warm earth and tucked his free hand beneath his head. "I can't blame you for not wanting to come," he said, closing his eyes. The sunlight filtering through the tree branches left patterns of light and shadow across his face.

"You can't?" I asked.

"Of course not. This isn't your home, and before coming here you didn't know us. I felt the same way when I first got here."

I hadn't really considered the fact that Miguel was not native to Guatemala. He was born and raised in New York. I wondered how he ended up here.

"Why are you here, Miguel, in Reu?" I asked. His face looked serene. I resisted the temptation to touch him, to trace the curve of his chin with my fingers.

He plucked a leaf off the lemon tree. "I wish I knew," he said. "This is Dora's home, her family. After my dad married her, I guess he wanted her to be where she felt comfortable."

"But this isn't your home," I said, "or your family."

"They're okay, I guess. I've gotten used to it."

"Have you?"

Miguel tossed the leaf aside and plucked another. He seemed contemplative.

"You've probably noticed that my dad hasn't been around the past few days," he said. "Not since the morning you overheard us arguing."

I recalled Dora saying something that day about taking Raul to the airport. I hadn't paid much attention, but now that Miguel mentioned it, I hadn't seen him come back.

"He flew out on another business trip. Won't be back for two weeks. I was mad because if he wasn't going to be here for Christmas, then I should at least be able to fly home and spend it with my mom. But he wouldn't listen. So, I'm stuck here with Dora. She's okay and everything, but—"

"But she's not your family." I finished Miguel's thought, and he nodded. So, that's what he and his father had been fighting about. I'm glad he finally felt he could confide in me. He raised the leaf and tried to balance it on my nose. We both laughed.

"Anyway," Miguel continued, "I think the real reason my dad moved me here was because he's gone on business so much, and dumping me on Dora is easier than being a responsible father."

His words were laced with cynicism—and sadness. He felt abandoned. No wonder he felt angry so much of the time, and why he resented how my father had, in a sense, abandoned his family for so long.

"That's what I meant when I said Guatemala isn't your home," added Miguel. "You didn't choose to come here. And it's not your fault your dad needed a reunion to pacify his own guilt."

Miguel was right. My dad had come here to patch things up with his family. But why did he have to pick now, the first anniversary of my mother's death, to repair the damage?

I watched Miguel for a few moments and studied his features—his lashes, the shape of his nose, the angle of his jawline.

"But here's the thing," I said, summoning what little courage I had. "Reu is kind of growing on me. You're *growing* on me."

Miguel looked at me for a long time before responding. "And...?" he asked expectantly.

What could I say to him? I should say that we were just friends—cousins—and that was enough. But now, being there next to him—how could I explain that the longer I was in Reu, the more I thought about him, that when I was near him I could hardly keep my heart from exploding out of my chest?

I lowered myself onto my elbow so that he and I were parallel, Miguel on his back, me on my side. Then, going against everything I had been telling myself for days, I leaned in and kissed him.

It felt just like the first time we kissed, only this time my entire body felt magnetic. I was drawn to him like a wave is drawn to shore, pulling me closer until our bodies were pressed together, the earth cradling us.

His lips opened, and his tongue searched for mine. God, he tasted good, and something electric sparked inside of me. Our hands skated across the fabric of our clothing. I could feel his muscles beneath his shirt. I kissed him harder, and he met my zeal with his own. And then I was the one on the ground and Miguel was leaning over me, his lips gliding across my throat.

At first, the sound of Abuela's front door opening didn't register. But the heavy steps of my father's shoes on the ceramic tile shot a warning through me like a siren blaring. But it was too late.

"Get away from her!"

Dad crossed the garden and grabbed Miguel by the arm, hauling him off me as I scrambled to my feet. I had never seen Dad like this before, outraged and out of control. He grabbed Miguel's shirt in his left fist and pulled back his right, preparing for the first punch. Miguel said nothing. He looked Dad square in the eye. Unafraid. Unashamed.

"Stop it!" I shouted. I couldn't help it, but I started to cry. Miguel may not have been afraid, but I was. "He didn't do anything!"

"I told you to watch out for him," Dad said, iron in his voice.

"It wasn't him. It was me," I said. "This was my fault." Dad's fist tightened, his eyes boring holes into Miguel. "You've got to believe me," I pleaded. "He didn't do anything wrong."

My father and Miguel stared at each other, each silently daring the other to make the first move. My Dad finally lowered his fist and shoved Miguel away from him. Then he turned to me. His voice was calmer now, but strained.

"Carly, go to your room."

"What?" His command took me by surprise. He hadn't sent me to my room since I was five years old. Why did he want me to leave? So I wouldn't witness what would happen next?

"No," I said. "No, I won't!"

His glare turned cold, but there was something else in his expression—regret.

"I said, go to your room."

I looked at Miguel, then to my father and back at Miguel again. I wanted to stay, but Miguel told me to go, not with words—with his eyes. Reluctantly, I turned away, sobbing. I ran to my room and slammed the door shut behind me.

Twenty-Four

I LAY ON MY BED WATCHING THE CLOCK'S HANDS click away time. An hour passed. Then two. My pillow was soaked with tears. I wondered what had happened between Miguel and my father. I felt sick inside thinking about how angry my father was.

The bedroom door opened, and a shadow fell across the clock's face, drawing my gaze toward the door. I expected to find my dad there, but it wasn't him.

"Papa Beto?"

My grandfather stood just inside my room, a plate of food in his hands. He carried it to the desk and set it down. The smell of baked chicken and fried *papas* made my mouth water.

Papa Beto pointed to the bed. I scooted over to make room for him to sit down. As he did so, he scratched at the gray stubble on his chin.

"*¿Qué pasa?*" he asked.

152

"Nothing's wrong. *Nada*," I lied. I wiped the tears from my cheeks with my hands and turned toward the wall. Above me the painting of the beach at sunset was unmercifully bright and colorful. Papa Beto waited as if he knew there was more inside me.

"Something *is* wrong," I admitted finally. "It's my father. I hate him! He didn't ask me if I wanted to come here. He made me come. Now he's threatened the only friend I have here. He even sent me to my room—this isn't even *my* room! This isn't my house or my country or my family! He's selfish! And I hate him!"

The anger exploded out of me like a volcano erupting. I couldn't control it. I hit my pillow with my fists and screamed. Then, the initial explosion over, I laid on my back and breathed deeply. Papa Beto was still sitting on my bed, watching me calmly. I had almost forgotten that he was there.

"I'm sorry," I said, feeling embarrassed about my outburst. Then a little laugh bubbled up my throat. "You don't understand me, do you? Here I am raving like a lunatic, and you don't have a clue what I'm saying." I sighed and smiled at my grandfather. His face was so kind, so compassionate, I could almost believe he understood me.

"I will say one thing," I told him, "you are a wonderful listener."

I turned my attention to the painting above my bed. That image—a moment of time held captive like a portal to the past. I reached up and touched it, somehow

153

expecting to feel sand between my fingers and the spray of saltwater on my skin. But I felt only the rough texture of acrylic on canvas.

"*¿Le gusta pintar?*" asked Papa Beto.

"*Sí.* I like the painting," I told him. "It's of Champerico, isn't it?"

Papa Beto nodded.

I tipped my head back so I could see the painting better. "It's no Monet," I added, "but there's something familiar about the way the artist sees things."

I waited for Papa Beto to respond. He was a quiet man. He hadn't said much to me since I arrived. I thought of the way I treated him when I first came here, as though I was better than him. I felt ashamed and wished that I could tell him so.

I sensed that he wanted me to continue talking, so I did.

"Sometimes when I lay here at night," I continued, "I imagine that I'm standing on that beach watching the sun set. It's as if I'm standing in the artist's shoes. No, not like that. More like the artist and I are the same person."

I laughed, suddenly self-conscious. "I'm rambling. Sorry. I do that sometimes."

Papa Beto stood up. He held out one of his hands, telling me to wait, then left the room. A few moments later he returned, carrying a long, narrow bundle. I sat up as he handed it to me.

The bundle was made of soft, yellow leather and was tied around the middle with a piece of string. I untied the string and unrolled it on my bed. There, tucked in a row of neat little pockets, were five paintbrushes. Each brush was made of fine bristles, some thin, some wide. I removed one of the brushes and turned the handle between my fingers. There were letters etched into the wood. Holding it close to see the small print, I read the words: ANTONIO PEREZ.

"My father's?" I asked, bewildered. Papa Beto smiled. He took the brush from my hand and held it up against the painting of Champerico, drawing the soft bristles across the length of the canvas.

"*Su papá lo pintó cuando era niño,*" he said.

"My dad painted that?" I was stunned. I never knew my father could paint. He never told me.

Papa Beto replaced the brush in its pocket and rolled up the leather. He carefully tied the band, then handed the bundle back to me.

"*Para usted,*" he said.

For you.

I accepted it, unsure of what to say. "*Gracias,*" was the best I could do.

I lost track of how many minutes passed after Papa Beto left the room. I sat on the edge of my bed with the leather bundle in my hands until the steam stopped rising from my food and the daylight outside my window dimmed to gray.

A light rap at my window drew me out of my daze. I looked at the window and saw a face staring back at me.

155

"Miguel!" I cried out in surprise. "What are you doing here?"

I slid open the window, and Miguel pulled himself through it into the room.

"You don't mind if I drop in, do you?" he asked.

"You shouldn't be here," I chided. "If my father finds you, he'll —"

"I can handle your father."

"He didn't hit you, did he?"

Miguel laughed, which set my mind at ease. No, as angry as Dad had been, he wouldn't strike anyone. Miguel pushed the clock and nativity set to the back of the desk and sat down.

"I came to make sure you're all right," he said.

"I'm fine," I told him, though I was not yet convinced that that was true. Miguel didn't seem convinced either.

"You've been crying," he said. He slid off the desk and onto the bed beside me. He wrapped his arm around my shoulder and spoke softly to me.

"Something's bothering you, more than just tonight. Is it that guy you keep seeing?"

"Sort of, but it's not just that. You wouldn't understand."

"How do you know?" Miguel bumped me playfully. "I opened up to you earlier, though how you managed to wheedle all that emotional mumbo jumbo out of me, I'll never know."

I couldn't help but laugh.

"C'mon," he added. "Give me a try."

I decided to take a chance on him. Besides, who else did I have to turn to?

"It's these dreams," I began. "I've actually been having them for months now. No, not dreams really— more like disjointed images. I can't really explain it," I answered, shaking my head in exasperation. "Sometimes they are just memories, glimpses of the past. But other times they are bizarre and creepy. My therapist gave me sleeping pills to keep them away. But I'm beginning to think the dreams are trying to tell me something, something I have forgotten."

I half expected Miguel to run out of the room to escape this insane person who suddenly had him captive, but he just sat there listening.

"They're about her," I said. "My mother. I keep playing that night over and over in my head. But it's all like Swiss cheese, filled with holes."

"What do you mean?"

I looked at Miguel. I couldn't expect him to understand. He hardly knew me, really. Until a little more than a week ago, I was just some face in a photograph. I wasn't even sure if he had known my mom had died. How much information did Dad's family have before he decided to reconnect with them?

"She died on Christmas Eve," I said. "It was snowing out. She had insisted on going out for one last gift. I didn't want to go. When we left the store, it was dark out. The roads were icy. A car swerved into our lane. I remember seeing the headlights. We tried to steer out of

157

its path, but the tires slid on the ice. There were loud, horrible sounds. I felt pain. I screamed. It was over in seconds. The next thing I remember was waking up in the hospital days later. They postponed my mom's funeral until I was strong enough to go in a wheelchair."

"I'm sorry, Carly," said Miguel. He sounded sincere, like he really cared, and I was glad he was there.

"Anyway," I continued, not wanting any pity, "not only do I have these weird dreams, but now that old guy keeps popping up everywhere. But I'm not even sure about that anymore."

Verbalizing everything made me feel worse than ever. I threw my hands up in exasperation. "All right, Miguel. I'm finished," I said. "You can run away now. Go on. Free yourself of the crazy girl before it's too late."

Obediently taking my cue, Miguel's expression turned serious. He let go of my hand to stroke invisible whiskers on his chin and adjust an imaginary monocle.

"I see," he said in a very bad German accent. "Every*vhere* you turn you see *dis* strange man, and now *dere* are images — and *ze* dreams!"

Miguel wrinkled his forehead as if in deep thought, then he broke into a hearty laugh.

"Carly, I think you need to give yourself a break," he said in his own voice. "You've been through a lot. But you're supposed to be on vacation, right?"

"I guess," I conceded.

"Then you need to do vacation things. Have some fun. Take your mind off things for a while. Maybe that's one reason your dad brought you here, to help you forget for a little while. I overheard your dad say something about going to Xela tomorrow. That should help."

"What's Xela?"

"A total tourist trap. You'll love it. We'll visit Zaculeu first and then double back to Xela. And in case you're wondering, Zaculeu is the site of an ancient city."

A small spark of hope began to burn inside me. Getting out of Reu for a day may be just what I needed.

"You're coming, too?" I asked hopefully.

"If your dad will let me, though I doubt he'd say no because he'd have to tell Dora what a villain I've been. Besides, someone has to look after you."

Miguel suddenly leaned in close and kissed me. It was brief but as wonderful as before. When he pulled away, he was smiling.

"As Dora would say," he continued, "*El que quiere pescado que se moje los huevos.* If you want to catch fish, you have to get your eggs wet."

"Meaning?"

Miguel scooped up my hand and laughed. "I have absolutely no idea, but I do know that you're not going anywhere without me."

Twenty-Five

THE ROAD TO ZACULEU WOUND ITS WAY through tropical mountain jungles, hugging the cliffs like a snake on a precarious limb. A thick mist hovered just above the ground, giving the entire mountain a surreal quality.

Dad borrowed Tio Raul's jeep for the day, but this time it was just the four of us: Dora, Dad, Miguel, and me. There was tension between Miguel and my dad, but neither said anything about the previous day. At least they were being civil to one another.

As we climbed higher and higher up the steep road, the temperature dropped in proportion to the altitude. Abuela had offered me a sweater before we left, and now I wished that I had accepted it. Even though I was wearing the only long sleeve shirt I had packed, it was all I could do to keep from shivering.

A deep valley fell away from the road on the left. Below us, a patch of bright colors caught my eye, and I

160

leaned forward to get a better look. Walking along a narrow path rising from the valley floor was a local family dressed in traditional attire. The mother and father each balanced a load of cut wood atop their heads. A young boy followed behind and waved as we passed by.

The ruins were not what I expected. I had envisioned something like Takalik Abaj, with its stelas and sprawling platforms, or Tikal, where temples two hundred feet high jutted above the dense Peten jungle. I had seen enough pictures of Tikal to imagine myself there, standing on a grassy field gazing heavenward toward the ancient ceremonial chambers atop dizzying flights of stone staircases.

But this was nothing like Tikal.

There was no grass here, at least not much of it. Some of the squat stone buildings that dotted the bare patch of earth were barely as tall as Abuela's house. While Dora and my dad were busy looking at a map on the far side of the site, Miguel climbed to the top of one of the monuments and held out his arms, shouting.

"I am Emperor Miguel! This is my kingdom!"

"Oh, really?" I said. "And since when do emperors carry water bottles and wear T-shirts that say *Kiss Me, I'm Spanish*?"

"Bow down before your emperor!"

"No way." I folded my arms and turned up my nose. Miguel leapt down the steps like a gazelle and swept me into his arms.

"Then I shall sacrifice you to the Gods!"

I pretended to put up a good fight, kicking and pounding his back with my fists. He carried me, nearly dropping me twice, up a short flight of steps and laid me on a flat rectangular stone.

"Let me go! Let me go!" I shouted, trying not to laugh.

"Shhh," said Miguel. "Sacrifices don't scream. They are willing participants. They want to die to appease the Gods."

"I don't believe that for one second," I said, but Miguel shushed me again. I lay as still as I could and tried to muffle my giggles while Miguel lifted a fist in the air, as if holding an imaginary knife.

"I dedicate the blood and body of this virgin to the Gods! I pray she is a worthy sacrifice."

As I lay there listening to Miguel's made up prayer, it occurred to me that this slab of stone had at one time really been an altar. Maybe ancient Mayan priests had really offered human sacrifices here. In my mind, I saw the scene — a man bound to the stone, struggling to get free as the priest plunged a dagger into his chest. I could hear the screams and see the blood spilling into the sand.

As Miguel's hand came down, suddenly this wasn't funny anymore. My mind reeled as images carved in stone came to life, gyrating in wild heathen ceremonies, and visions of dead men, their blood bathing the altar on which they lay, made my heart beat like a herd of wild horses.

"Stop," I said, but Miguel didn't hear me. His imaginary knife sliced across each of my wrists.

I repeated the word. "Stop!"

The knife sliced across my throat.

"STOP!"

This time he heard me. He was laughing now. I sat up, surprised at my own reaction, and quickly climbed down the stones to the arena. It wasn't until I was on level ground that I realized I was shaking.

"What?" asked Miguel once he'd caught up with me. "I didn't scare you, did I?"

"Of course not," I told him, because how could I explain what I had experienced up there? He wouldn't have understood. He would have thought I was crazy.

"Are you feeling okay, Carly?"

"I am a little cold," I said. "Why?"

"You look pale. Probably the altitude. Hey, you've never seen where the Mayans played ball."

I noticed that Dad and Dora were now standing where Miguel and I had just been. Dora was lying on the altar and Dad was snapping pictures with his camera. I wished that Miguel would reach for my hand the way he normally did, but after Dad's tirade the other day, we kept a respectful distance from each other while in Dad's sight.

I followed Miguel to a pair of long rectangular structures that were flat on top. The sides facing each other were sloped. We climbed to the top of one of them and sat down.

"This is where the spectators would sit to watch the game," Miguel explained. "It was kind of like an ancient version of soccer, except that the losers were sacrificed. Which reminds me," he added, "I have a game tomorrow morning. Maybe you can watch me play."

I told him I'd love to. Then, with Dad and Dora busy elsewhere, he took my hand.

I looked out over the narrow game field and imagined the players as they must have looked thousands of years ago. Their skin, bronzed by the intense Mesoamerican sun, glistened with perspiration as they bounced their ball against one another's bodies. Then, as if I was really there, I heard the cheers of the crowd each time a player scored a point. I saw the blood spurting from the chest of the loser sacrificed to their Gods.

The present dissolved into the past. This moment, today, was fleeting, gone in a single breath, but the past, I realized, was eternal. These stone monuments testified to that. I couldn't help but think of what happened a year ago: the noise, the lights, the accident. Would those memories torment me forever?

Being here among these ancient ruins, I felt as though I had traveled back in time. I stood where men and women stood before me over a thousand years ago. I touched the same stones and walked the same paths. Closing my eyes, I felt the people sitting beside me. I heard their laughter, smelled the pungent scent of their bodies pressing close to me, and the sharp stench of blood carried on the breeze. When I opened my eyes, I was sure I would see them. I would have changed — my body transformed to look like them. I was one of them.

Slowly, I opened my eyes. The field before me was bare and the stone walls decaying. I let out a slow, disappointed breath.

"You two want a soda?"

Dad called up to me, holding two frosty bottles of Orange Crush in his hands. Miguel and I clambered down to him and took the drinks, grateful for liquid refreshment.

"It's time to go," Dad said. "Next stop Xela."

As we headed back to the jeep, I couldn't shake the feeling that I was leaving something of myself behind. Though maybe that wasn't it at all. Maybe something was leaving *with* me, and the thought of that possibility made me shiver.

Twenty-Six

WE DOUBLE-BACKED ALONG THE ROAD we had taken earlier and headed toward Xela. I was anxious to leave Zaculeu and its sacrifices behind. It was one place I never wanted to see again.

"Do you know the story of Xela?" Dad asked, breaking a long silence. "Xela has always been home to the Mayans. The Quiché called it Xelajú. In the year 1524, the Spaniards, led by conquistador Pedro de Alvarado, met an army of Quiché right here in these highlands."

Dad's expression grew increasingly animated. His eyes widened and his voice deepened. He loved to tell stories.

"Legend has it," he continued, "that Alvarado killed the leader of the Quiché, Tecún Umán, in hand to hand combat. A gold and green Quetzal bird landed on the fallen king's body, staining its breast red with his blood."

"Alvarado called his soldiers to come see this beautiful bird, the most beautiful bird he had ever seen anywhere in the world. In its honor, they named this place Quetzaltenango."

"But to this day," Dora chimed in, "the natives still prefer their own name of Xela."

That was the second story I'd heard about how the Quetzal got its red breast, and they both involved blood.

As Dora completed Dad's story, the jeep came around a bend and the road straightened. Xela appeared suddenly as though it was the legendary city of El Dorado itself materializing before our eyes. We stopped at a turnout in the road.

"*La Ciudad de los Altos*," said Dad reverently. "The City of the Heights."

We stood at the crest of a valley, which cradled the city of Xela like a brilliant green tapestry suspended from the mountains and volcanoes that surrounded it. The city itself sprawled out in every direction, criss-crossed by a network of avenues. This was not the village I had imagined, but a thriving metropolis.

The road continued downward into the heart of Xela. The colonial architecture of the buildings took my breath away. Dad introduced each structure by name as we passed: Banco Occidental, Teatro Municipal, Casa de Cultura. Each building was more magnificent than the one preceding it, adorned with lofty scalloped pillars and triangular pinnacles reminiscent of the sixteenth and seventeenth centuries in which the earliest of these buildings had been constructed.

But the one that impressed me most was the Espíritu Santo Cathedral. Three elegantly rounded spires, paying homage to the Father, the Son, and the Holy Ghost, capped the immense five hundred-year-old edifice. I pleaded with Dad to park the car so I could get out and take some pictures.

Miguel dashed through Central Park towards the Cathedral. I tried to keep up, but my leg was giving me trouble, and I was also feeling a little dizzy. As Miguel had suggested earlier, it was probably just the altitude. Despite my slow pace, I managed to arrive only a few seconds after Miguel.

We stood there for a moment admiring the cathedral. From its base, it looked enormous. The sheer size of it sent my head into a whirl and I had to look away and close my eyes to get my bearings again. But suddenly, I wasn't in Xela. I was at home, in the snow.

No. I was beside our Christmas tree, shattered glass all around me, glistening in the blinking lights. Then I was outside again and felt the sting of ice on my face, and there were red lights blinking. On. Off. On. Off.

"Dora wants to walk to the Mercado de la Democracia and do some shopping."

Dad's voice jerked me out of my dream. Only it couldn't have been a dream. It was the middle of the day, and I was just standing there.

"After that, we can grab something to eat before visiting the zoo at the far end of the city."

How long had Dad been talking? When had he appeared beside me?

Miguel replied that he could use some lunch. My stomach had started grumbling before we even entered the city, but I wasn't sure if it was from hunger or something else.

"Do they have any good restaurants here?" I asked, pretending nothing out of the ordinary had happened. Nor did I want to dampen the day with a little stomach ache.

Dad looked at me with mock offense. "Only the best restaurants in Guatemala!" he said.

"How about a Big Mac?" Miguel asked.

"They have a McDonald's here?" I said. Whatever that momentary lapse was, it was over now. Strange things could happen, I guess, when you're hungry and seven thousand feet above sea level.

Dad rolled his eyes. "Yes, they have a McDonald's here. We're not completely archaic, you know."

"I could use some fries," said Miguel, "and a vanilla shake about now."

Dad clapped his hands together and started walking back toward the car where Dora waited. "It's settled then," he called over his shoulder. "Burgers for everyone—but shopping first."

The Mercado de la Democracia was like the market in Reu, but on a much grander scale. Dad joined Miguel on a nearby bench and announced that they would wait for the women there.

"It's just like in the United States," said Dora, linking elbows with me. "Men hate to shop."

The shops were arranged linearly, connected by high curved archways so that patrons could move freely from one shop to the next without having to go outside. Dora and I stopped first at a clothier to admire the now familiar embroidery and colorful weaves of fabric.

"Their cloth is so beautiful," I said after finding a jacket similar to the one I had seen in Reu. Dora removed it from its hanger and told me to try it on. I obeyed, and the jacket fit perfectly from the length of the sleeves to the cut of the shoulder. I ran my fingers along the thin stripes of green, purple and blue that ran vertically down the front, then I glanced at the back in the full-length mirror on the wall. There, in bold shades of emerald and scarlet, was the Quetzal, its majestic wings spread in flight.

"It's yours," said Dora decisively. "I recall you drooling over one just like it when you first arrived. The moment I laid eyes on this one, I knew it had to be yours."

I felt overwhelmed by Dora's generosity. "I can't accept this," I told her, removing the jacket. "I don't deserve it."

"Let me tell you something, Carlita," answered Dora. "You do deserve this. You deserve to be happy." She said it earnestly, as if the words bore more significance than a simple gift warranted. There was something more behind it, but before I could think about it further, she helped me back into the jacket and straightened the shoulders. "Perhaps this one moment of happiness will be the first of many," she added with a smile.

Dora's words weighed on me. Maybe it was guilt that she and my father hadn't seen each other for twenty years and now she was trying to make it up to me. But somehow even that didn't seem right. I thought of my leg and my permanent limp. Did she feel sorry for me? Or was there something more?

"I – I don't know what to say," I stammered.

Dora shrugged. "*Gracias* will do just fine."

I tried to swallow the lump in my throat. I wanted to tell Dora how much I appreciated everything she had done for me during my stay in Reu. I wanted to tell her that I was glad I came, and that most of all, I loved her. But the only sound that came out of my mouth was a meek, "*Gracias, Tía.*"

Dora gazed into my eyes as if searching for something there.

"*Te quiero.* But Carly," she said softly, "are you feeling all right?" She put a hand to my forehead. "You feel warm, Mija. Maybe we should go now, take you home to rest."

"No, I'm fine," I protested. "Really."

I smiled widely to convince her. She narrowed her eyes, skeptical of my performance. But then she nodded.

"If you say so," she said. Then, with renewed enthusiasm, she added, "I must spend some *dinero*! I spied some pottery in the next room, and over there are the most amazing carvings. Maybe you could find something to take home with you, to remind you of Guate."

Dora paid for the jacket and then disappeared through the archway to the shop next door. I turned my attention to a hand-carved nativity scene displayed on a nearby table. It resembled the set Miguel had given me, each figure modestly hewn from light-colored wood. As I held up each piece, I thought of the crystal angel that had adorned the top of our tree my entire life. Its details were intricate and fine, unlike the wooden angel I now held in my hands, with its plain brown robe and flawed wings.

When I replaced the angel on the table, I realized that my hands were trembling. I felt chilled to the bone and pulled the Quetzal jacket tight around me. Turning to leave, I glimpsed movement out of the corner of my eye. My pulse raced and my body grew rigid with fear. I turned slowly toward the shop's outer door—and stifled a scream.

Twenty-Seven

IN THE NEXT SHOP OVER, Tía Dora was browsing a table piled high with pottery. She was inspecting a miniature clay tea set glazed in green when I ran up to her.

"Help me!" I didn't care that everyone's eyes were on me. "Help me, please!"

Dora took me by the shoulders and looked me squarely in the eyes. "Mija, what has happened? Why are you afraid?"

She put the back of her hand against my cheek. I was breathing so fast I could barely speak.

"In the shop! He's in the shop!"

"Who, Carlita? Who's in the shop?"

I didn't answer her. Instead, I bolted through the outer door and ran to my father. He rose from his bench the moment he saw me and caught me in his arms.

"What's wrong? You look like you've seen a ghost," he said.

Dora followed me out of the Mercado. Miguel hurried over as well. I grabbed his arm.

"Miguel, it's him!" I was shouting now but I didn't care who heard me. "That man I told you about. He's here!"

"You mean the guy from the plane? Raisin Face?"

I nodded frantically.

"Remember what we decided," he reminded me. "He's not real. He's just an illusion."

"He *is* real! He's following me!" I knew I sounded hysterical. But I didn't care.

"Calm down, honey," said Dad, the tension in his voice increasing. "What are you talking about? Who is following you?"

Dora interrupted. "I think she's ill, Tony. She has a fever."

I darted my eyes toward the Mercado and back to my father's face. Then I saw him standing beside an ice cream cart only yards away. He gazed at me with those sad eyes of his, his wrinkled face looking more haggard and dismal than ever. As I watched him, he turned his head, first to one side and then the other, as if telling me there was no way out, no escape.

I tried to pull free from my father's grasp. I wanted to run. I wanted to run and hide.

"What do you want from me?!" I screamed. Everyone in the marketplace was watching me now, but I didn't care. I needed to get away. I needed to break away and run. "Why are you following me?!"

Raisin Face looked at me with the same solemn expression as before, shaking his head slowly back and forth. I wrenched myself free from my father's hands and took off, desperate to get away. I heard my family calling after me and the sound of footsteps behind me, but I could not be sure it wasn't Raisin Face pursuing me.

I kept running. I tripped, and a sharp pain shot up through my leg, but I kept running. I was heading back towards the cathedral. In ancient times, cathedrals were places of refuge, of safety. Maybe I would be safe there. But as I neared the Cathedral door, he was already there waiting for me. How had he gotten there so fast? How had he passed me without my seeing him?

I turned to my right, ready to run again, but there he was, not two feet in front of me. I spun back, and he was there. He was everywhere—all around me!

My entire body shuddered, and tears cascaded down my cheeks.

The world spun around me, Raisin Face orbiting like a menacing planet.

Someone shouted my name, but the voice was too distant—a hazy dream.

I couldn't run anymore.

I couldn't escape.

My legs buckled, and I collapsed as the light around me faded to black.

Twenty-Eight

I WOKE UP WITH A JOLT, as if lightening had struck me. The muted sounds of voices became suddenly clear, distinguished from the noise of rainfall on the roof above.

"Carly? Carly, are you all right?"

I felt the warmth of someone's hand on mine. I opened my eyes slowly and saw my father leaning over me, his face pale with worry.

"She's coming to. *Está volviendo,*" he said, relief in his voice.

I was in a bare room lying on a cot of some kind. Tía Dora stood behind my father, her hands clasped as if in prayer. I felt dizzy and a little nauseous.

"What happened?" I asked.

Dad patted my hand reassuringly. "You fainted."

I reached up to touch my temple, which throbbed painfully.

"You hit your head when you fell." Miguel was speaking now. "But the doctor said it's nothing serious."

"Doctor? No doctors…"

"It's all right," said Dad. "You've just got a touch of the flu. We're going to take you home now."

I tried to sit up but Dad held my shoulders down. "Lie down, Carly. There's no hurry."

"I don't want to lie down," I protested, but I felt weak and tired. I could barely utter any more words. I managed only three.

"Is he gone?"

But I was asleep before anyone could answer.

It was dark outside when I woke up again. I was back in my room in Abuela's house. The lamp on my desk was on, and the clock said it was well past midnight. I no longer felt dizzy, and the ache in my stomach was gone. But I was weak and a little shaky.

With some effort, I got out of bed. I stood in my doorway hoping someone might happen to come by to check on me, but the house was quiet, and I was alone. Sleep had left me. How would I pass the time until morning?

I decided to draw.

I took out my art box and limped to the garden where Abuela's lemon tree was bathed in moonlight, silver glinting off every leaf. I sat down at the edge of the veranda and put the box beside me. Opening it, I took

177

out a pencil and the pad of paper and turned to the ever-familiar smeared image that would not find a shape for itself. I put the pencil to it, but my hand refused to move. No matter how hard I tried, no lines would come.

Frustration bubbled up inside me, and I snapped the pencil in two. I tore the gray image out and ripped it into a hundred tiny pieces. A breeze rustled through the leaves of the tree, so I held out my hands and let the breeze carry the pieces across the garden where they drifted down to the earth—like snowflakes.

Purged of that shapeless mess, I went to the kitchen and got a glass of water. Then I returned to my spot on the veranda. A new white sheet of paper lay open there. I took out the tempera cakes, arranging them around me like a rainbow. I dipped my brush into the water and swirled it against the blue paint. Then I put the brush to paper.

My strokes felt smooth and sure, and I was surprised at how easily it all came back to me. I guess I thought I should have forgotten how to paint by now. When I was a kid, I took piano lessons but stopped after a couple of years. Recently, when I sat down at a friend's piano, I couldn't remember a thing. But this was different.

I swished my brush around in the water. Then I selected another color: green. My fingers and hand tingled, and energy flowed up my arm into my shoulder. It was a familiar feeling, one I had first felt years ago as a young girl.

I had always enjoyed painting, as most kids do, but I wasn't any good at it. Then one day, Mom stood behind me and laid her hand on mine. The warmth from her skin traveled through my arm into my body as she gently guided my hand across the paper. The brush glided along like a swan on water. Eventually, I let my hand go limp. She lifted it, dipped the brush in the water, touched it to the paint, and we continued on floating, gliding, soaring across the page. At one point, I could not tell which hand was hers and which was mine. They were one hand.

Now, sitting here on Abuela's veranda, I could feel her with me, guiding me again—her hand on mine, her warmth, her energy, flowing into me. I wanted this moment to go on forever, but like all mortals trapped in earthbound bodies, exhaustion soon forced me to lay down my brush. I put away my art supplies and snapped the box shut before heading back to bed. As I lay in the dark, I felt a keen sense of satisfaction.

I had painted again.

Twenty-Nine

IN THE MORNING, I FELT MUCH BETTER. My strength had returned, and the throbbing in my head had subsided to a mild ache.

My first thought was the realization that today was Christmas Eve, the anniversary of my mother's accident. An all too familiar feeling of grief threatened to consume me, but I couldn't let it. I had to keep occupied today.

I could hear Abuela busy in the kitchen, so I ventured out of my room to see if breakfast was ready. As usual, Papa Beto and my dad were sitting at the table. After yesterday's ordeal, I didn't feel like being interrogated, so I put on the best face I could. Dad raised his eyes as I approached.

"Look who's awake. How are you feeling?" he asked.

"Better," I told him. And it was true. Whatever had hit me yesterday was gone now. "In fact, I'm famished."

"Abuela's just starting on breakfast. Should be ready in twenty minutes or so."

"That's fine," I said. "In the meantime, I'm going to take a little walk and get some fresh air."

Dad eyed me suspiciously. "Miguel's not home," he said, "if seeing him is what you had in mind."

"I wasn't planning on going to Dora's," I replied casually. And that was true too. I already knew Miguel wouldn't be home. He was playing in a soccer game this morning. I remember him mentioning it that day at Takalik Abaj, and yesterday he'd brought it up again and invited me to come.

As I started for the door, Dad asked, "Are you sure you're all right? Last night you weren't yourself. You kept saying *he* was after you. Who did you mean?"

"It was nothing," I answered hastily. "Just the fever, I guess. But I'm fine, now. Really. You don't have to worry."

Dad nodded, satisfied, and then turned back to his paper. I went outside.

A few minutes later, I arrived at the soccer stadium. Miguel's team was on the field warming up. The bleachers were full of spectators, and I had to climb nearly to the top to find an empty seat. I wish there was some way to let him know I was here, but I didn't want to distract him.

The game began. Almost immediately, Miguel got possession of the ball and took it down toward the net, but a player in blue stole the ball and passed it to another

181

on his team, who, twenty seconds later, scored the first goal.

Miguel looked angry but seemed ready to continue when several of his teammates gathered around him. I recognized some of them from before. The fat-faced boy with the small nose, Tomás, was shouting at Miguel. I was too far away to hear exactly what was being said, but I could tell it wasn't good.

Miguel shouted back, and then Tomás shoved him. Miguel clenched his hands into fists, and it looked as though a fight would break out. But a referee intervened. Miguel angrily pulled off his jersey. Then, throwing it to the ground, he stormed off the field. Another player was called in to take his place. The game continued as if nothing had happened.

The game had barely begun and Miguel had left. What did this mean? Had he quit? Had his teammates kicked him out? I carefully made my way down the bleachers, trying not to trip over my bum leg. Eventually, I reached level ground and headed outside to find Miguel. I hoped he hadn't left yet. If he had, maybe I'd find him at Dora's.

As I exited the stadium, I spotted Miguel leaning shirtless against the wall. But he wasn't alone. Tomás's sister, Maria, was with him. Miguel was angry, his eyes burning with rage. She spoke softly to him, maybe trying to calm him down after what had happened, but he seemed to be ignoring her, looking off somewhere else.

She stepped close to him and laid her hands against his bare chest. The gesture was intimate, personal. Miguel's eyes, still full of fury, shifted to her face. He reached up with both hands and grabbed her wrists.

Then suddenly, she kissed him.

It wasn't a long kiss, but it wasn't quick either. I should have looked away. I shouldn't care what Miguel did. He and I hardly knew each other; I had no claim on him. He'd made no promises, no commitments to me. I had no right to feel the way I did. But I couldn't help it. Jealousy surged through my veins like hot oil, burning me from the inside out.

Maria pressed closer to Miguel, but just then, he looked up. When he saw me, he froze, a look of shock on his face.

"Carly?" he said, but I didn't answer him. Instead, I ran.

Thirty

THE CELEBRATION OF OUR ARRIVAL was repeated that afternoon. As the day wore on, more relatives showed up, and Dad greeted them all with open arms and unlimited coconuts. There were two people noticeably absent, however. Tio Raul, who was away on business, and Miguel. He had called me several times over the past few hours, but I refused to speak to him. Rather than keep getting the missed call notifications, I just turned my phone off.

I tried to enjoy the party, but without Miguel, I felt out of place again. Wanting to avoid the barrage of kisses that would certainly come with announcing my retirement to bed, I shuffled along the edge of the walkway where the shadows were deepest and headed for my room. Soon I was safe inside, and I closed the door, hoping no one had noticed my departure. From the garden, swells of laughter rose and fell like the tide, washing over me like the waves of Champerico, the waves that stole my hat and carried it far away.

After a few minutes, there was a light rap on the door. Dora's face appeared in the doorway.

"Are you ill again, Mija?"

For a split second, I considered lying and saying I had a headache so that no one would bother me the rest of the evening, but I couldn't bring myself to say anything to Dora but the truth.

"No, Tía," I told her.

"You know, Carly, it is considered impolite to leave a room full of guests without saying *buenas noches*." She tipped her head to one side as she studied my face. "Unless it is for a very good reason."

"I'm not up for company tonight." I sat on the end of the bed. Dora sat beside me.

"I see," she said, resting her hands in her lap. "Perhaps it is not our company you are not up to. I've sensed friction between you and Tony. You are angry with him for bringing you to this place, to these people who are so foreign to you."

"No—" I replied hastily. "I mean yes, I admit I was angry at first, but things are different now. I like it here, but..."

"But you are still angry," Dora finished my sentence, translating my thoughts into words.

"Yes," I said. "I wanted Christmas to be the same as always. I *needed* it to be the same. But when I look out into the garden and see my dad smiling, laughing—"

185

I couldn't continue. The fury in me swelled.

Dora wrapped her arm around my shoulder.

"Maybe it's time to let go of some of that anger," she said. "Your father loves you very much. He would not have brought you here unless he believed it was for the best."

I wanted to let go of my anger, but doing so would leave me vulnerable. A new emotion crept into my heart, and this feeling hurt more than anger ever did.

"It was one year ago," I said, barely audibly, "a year ago tonight since my mom died. I wanted to be home, in *our* home. Instead, my dad is here having the time of his life, as if it doesn't even matter."

Dora gave me a gentle squeeze, but she said nothing. She just let me say what I needed to say.

"I miss the snow," I whispered. "I miss my Christmas tree." I fought against the tears, but it was a losing battle. "I miss my mom."

Tears fell from Dora's eyes too. She buried her face in my hair and kissed the top of my head.

"I know you miss her, Mija," she whispered softly. "I know."

Thirty-One

I LAID IN MY BED until the painting on my wall was too dim to see in the fading light. No matter how hard I tried to fall asleep, sleep would not come. I was tempted to take my pills, but I had gone four days without them. If keeping my mind clear meant no rest, then so be it.

I wanted to go for a walk, but if I left my room I ran the risk of being noticed by Abuela's guests. So instead, I pushed aside the nativity set, climbed onto the desk, and opened the window. Then I carefully lowered myself to the ground outside.

The moon was partially hidden behind clouds, and its light was barely enough to illuminate my way. I decided to go to the cemetery. That little chapel where Miguel and I had found refuge from a rainstorm seemed the perfect spot to be alone, but the cemetery gate was locked. I grabbed hold of the bars and shook them like a condemned prisoner. The metal rattled. I was debating whether or not to search for another way in when I spied a group of three men standing at the corner sharing a bottle of whiskey between them. The noise of the gate had attracted their attention. The men watched me, a greedy look in their eyes. One wiped his mouth with his sleeve and nodded in my direction.

Miguel's warning came back to me, that it wasn't safe to come here at night. I turned back for Abuela's, but when I heard footsteps following me, alarms went off in my head, and I chided myself for being so careless.

As I approached the corner before Abuela's house, I dared a glance back, but I saw no one. Maybe the footsteps had been my imagination. I honestly didn't trust myself anymore. I paused and allowed myself a moment to breathe.

Suddenly, two hands grabbed my arms. I screamed and tried to run, but the grip on me tightened.

"Whoa! Wait a sec!"

It was Miguel's voice.

I stopped struggling and looked into his face. Relief washed over me. I was so grateful to see him, I nearly threw my arms around him—until I remembered how angry I was.

"What the hell are you doing out here?" he snapped at me. His tone was unexpectedly sharp.

I pushed him away. "I was about to ask you the same question!"

"It's late, Carly," said Miguel, fuming. "What were you thinking, leaving the house alone?"

"I wanted some time to myself," I said icily.

Miguel let out a frustrated breath. "You do know that your dad will kill you when he finds you missing."

"How do you know I'm missing? Maybe I told him I was going out."

"Right. And I'm Santa Claus."

I couldn't take listening to him anymore. I would rather have faced an entire house full of annoying relatives than him at that moment.

"I gotta go," I said, abruptly turning to leave, but he took my arm again, not hard. Just enough to keep me from storming off.

"I've been trying to call you."

"I turned off my phone."

"Listen," he continued, exasperated. "I know what you think you saw this morning —"

"Oh? What *did* I see?"

His face reddened. "You saw Maria kiss me," he said, "but it wasn't what you think."

"Wasn't it?" I couldn't believe it. I saw the kiss with my own eyes. Miguel saw me see him! How could he deny it?

He exhaled loudly and pushed the hair away from his eyes. "Look, Maria's been hitting on me for months. I try to be polite because her brother is the captain of my team."

I'd had enough. I finally snapped. "So, kissing beautiful girls is being polite in Guatemala?"

What was I doing? Miguel had never made any sort of commitment to me. He was free to kiss whomever he pleased. I looked at Miguel and could swear a smile was hiding behind his otherwise stern expression.

"Okay," he said, "I concede that she did in fact kiss me, but I did not kiss her back. She took me by surprise. If you had stuck around a little longer you might have seen me push her away."

What had I seen? Miguel had just stormed out of the stadium. He was angry and upset. Maria stood close to him, too close, but he wasn't looking at her. Like he hardly noticed she was there. Then she put her hands on his chest. He noticed her then, but his expression was hard, not how you'd expect a boy in love to respond.

Then I thought of the way he looked at me, his eyes totally focused on mine, his expression gentle and caring. That was not how he had looked at Maria.

How could I have been so stupid?

Miguel took a deep breath. His expression relaxed, but his focus on me sharpened. Then he slid his hand down my arm and interlaced his fingers with mine. "Maria is pretty, but I could never be with her."

"Why not?" I asked, that familiar warmth spreading through me.

"For one thing," he said, his smile finally making an appearance, "girls who throw themselves at me aren't my type."

"There's been more than one?"

Miguel laughed. "No. I just meant I'm not interested in Maria, never have been."

"Oh."

"The other reason," Miguel continued, "is because I've fallen for *you*."

He leaned toward me, paused as if waiting to make sure I wouldn't protest, and then kissed me gently on the lips. I closed my eyes and savored his touch, all the anger I'd felt just a minute ago melting away. When he stopped, I yearned for him to kiss me again, but he didn't.

Maria kissed Miguel, but he did not kiss her back. He didn't even like her that way. Somehow, I knew he was telling the truth. I had no reason to doubt him.

"In any case," he said, wrapping his arms around me, "I'm sorry about the misunderstanding. Believe me, I chewed Maria out after you left. I told her to stay away from me — for good."

I felt so relieved and happy to know how Miguel really felt about me. Like nothing in the world could ever go wrong again.

"What did happen at the game this morning?" I asked. "It had hardly begun when you walked out."

Miguel went quiet for a moment, but then he looked at me. "Tomás accused me of being distracted and threatened to throw me off the team if I didn't straighten up. I don't need that kind of crap, so I quit."

"You quit? But you love soccer!"

"I'll find a new team. I don't need them anyway. I don't like who I am when I'm with them. You helped me to see that."

Miguel touched my cheek, sending satisfying shivers all through me.

"But Tomás was right," he continued. "I *was* distracted. I was worried about you, wondering if you were feeling better, wondering what you really saw in Xela. And I was thinking about my parents. It's Christmas," he added, sadly, "and I'm here alone."

It made sense that he was distracted, I realized. His parents were both in the states and had left him here with Dora, with no real family of his own. No wonder he was so angry this morning and couldn't focus on his game. I felt for him and wished I could fix everything, but I couldn't.

Miguel drew me closer to him. "So, you still haven't answered my question."

I snaked my arms around Miguel's shoulders. I wanted him to kiss me again. "What question?"

"Why are you here?"

"I told you, I wanted to be alone."

"Ah, that's right. I suppose half of Reu is in Abuela's garden right now celebrating."

I nodded. "And what about you?" I asked. "What are you doing here? How did you know where to find me?"

"It just so happens that I was on my way to see you when I spied a certain young lady crawling out of her window. Reu is no place to be wandering around alone at night, unless you're feeling suicidal. So, I followed you here to make sure you were okay."

I gave Miguel a playful shove. "You sneak!"

"Yeah, but I'm a handsome sneak."

"Says who?"

He kissed me again, gentle but assured. There was no doubt he cared about me, no doubt at all.

"Tonight is the final night of Las Posadas," he said. "Are you feeling up to going?"

The last night of the Christmas celebrations! The night Mary and baby Jesus are finally welcomed into the inn.

"Yes!" I said enthusiastically. "Let's go now before we miss the whole thing."

"Wait, wait!" Miguel laughed. He took me by the shoulders and held me back at arms' length. "We can't just go without your father knowing where you are. You snuck out, remember? Go back to Abuela's and wait for me. I have to get the firecrackers from my house. I'll meet you in fifteen minutes. All right?"

He took my hand and started leading me toward Abuela's, but I resisted.

"What if I don't want to go back?" I asked. "What if I want to stay here with you? What if I want to stay in Reu forever and never go home to California?"

Miguel faced me and took both my hands in his. The earnest expression on his face took me by surprise.

"Listen, Carly," he began, "I care about you more than I've cared about anyone in a long time and hope that maybe we'll see each other again one day. But your dad doesn't approve of me."

"I don't think that's it," I said. "I think he's just afraid."

"Afraid of me?"

"Afraid of facing what he left behind a long time ago. Afraid that it's too late to go back."

"It's never too late, Carly." He kissed me one last time. But then the playfulness was back. "And what about you?" he asked.

"What about me?"

"How do you feel about this place, about *us*?"

"I'm not sure," I said. "When I first came here, I wanted nothing more than to be home. And I admit, I still want that. But now I'm torn. I do like it here, and I like being with you."

Miguel pushed the mop of hair out of his face. He was always doing that, and I loved that about him.

"Well, I'm glad to know I've bewitched you," he said. "But right now, you've got to get back. Your dad will wonder where you are."

I allowed Miguel to lead me back to Abuela's. I slid open my window, then watched Miguel saunter off down the street. More clouds had gathered overhead, blocking most of what little moonlight there was. Only a few streaks of silver lay in disorganized patterns on the ground. I was sitting on the windowsill with my legs still hanging outside when a movement in the shadow of a palm tree caught my attention.

"Miguel?" I called out, but then I realized that I had watched Miguel walk away in the other direction. My blood ran cold as the figure stepped out of the shadow into a pale patch of light.

Raisin Face!

I held still and tried not to breathe. *Had he seen me*, I wondered? It was so dark I couldn't be sure, but after a moment he turned and began walking in the same direction Miguel had gone. My heart pounded against my ribs. My first impulse was to get through that window and lock it tight behind me, but if I did that, how long would he go on tormenting me? Would I ever figure out who he was or why I kept seeing him?

I had a decision to make: go back into my room, or follow him.

I slid the window shut behind me and slipped quietly into the streets of Reu.

Thirty-Two

I FOLLOWED RAISIN FACE past the cemetery and the soccer stadium. A few minutes later, he walked through Miguel's neighborhood and past his house. Through the window, I could see Miguel rummaging in a closet, probably looking for the firecrackers. I considered giving up the chase and knocking on his door, but I continued on instead.

We reached the end of one street and turned down another. Soon, we'd left the familiar part of town. The streets were filled with people laughing, singing, and burning firecrackers in celebration of the birth of Christ. It became increasingly difficult to distinguish Raisin Face from the others in the crowd, but I managed to keep him in my sights.

On and on we went, down one street and up another. Sometimes he seemed to blend into the shadows. When that happened, I stopped and waited, scanning the darkness for signs of movement. Twice I thought I'd lost him, but then I spotted him shifting between scraps of light. He kept moving forward, and so did I.

Then...

Pop! Pop! Pop!

The air suddenly crackled with thousands of explosions from all over the city, like gunfire, like the world shattering all around me. I looked at my phone. It was midnight, the climax of the night's festivities. It had been hours since I'd left Abuela's. How had so much time passed?

During this pursuit, my mind had been alive with electric connections snapping and popping in my brain. Who was this man? Was he real or just some phantom of my imagination? I had to find out. After that day when I saw him in the cemetery, I had come to believe that my mind was playing tricks on me, sometimes twisting real faces into his face, other times conjuring him out of thin air like a magician's illusion.

But why would my brain betray me like that? I didn't *feel* crazy, but then how do crazy people feel? When you are living in your own fantasy, maybe that world is as real to you as other people's worlds are to them. Can the insane ever really know if they are insane, or are they convinced that they are the normal ones and everyone else around them is nuts?

While my mind spun around these thoughts, suddenly the sky broke open, and water deluged Reu, as though angels were throwing buckets of water down from heaven. Dora had mentioned the tropical storm that was screwing with the weather and had hoped it would pass by Christmas. But now the rain fell so hard I could barely see through it.

The firecrackers ceased, and the crowds retreated into their houses. The thick curtain of gray gave the world a smeared, hazy look. Simple objects, like houses, trees, and people lost their distinction, their lines blending into one fuzzy picture—like the shapeless image in my sketchpad.

The temperature dropped too. Maybe it was because my hair and clothes were saturated with water, but I began to shiver. The rain burst against the rooftops, and water sprayed off the walls like shrapnel. The streets quickly filled with water, and torrents of it flowed around and between my legs.

Then I realized he was gone again.

I stopped, waiting for him to reappear. My mind, however, would not stop its constant motion. Had I lost him for good? I worried that I had, but no. There! Movement in the shadows!

I started forward, ready to pursue him again, but then the shadow abruptly halted and turned.

If my heart did not stop beating, I know my lungs stopped breathing because I held my breath as the man started walking toward me. He had seen me. He knew I was there and was coming for me.

I wanted to run, run far away and never look back. But something in my brain told my feet to stay put. So, I stayed. I stood still, forcing myself to take one breath after another. *Breathe*, I told myself, *breathe*.

The man approached, and the closer he came the more distinct his lines became. Soon I could distinguish his head, arms, legs. Then I could see the outline of his shirt and his jeans. I saw his hair, soaked and hanging in his face.

I caught my breath again, waiting for that scarred visage. But when he was close enough for me to reach out and touch him, I saw that it wasn't Raisin Face at all.

It was my father.

Thirty-Three

"CARLY?" SAID DAD, rain spilling down his features. "Carly! I've been looking everywhere for you. I called you a million times, but it kept going to voicemail."

I remembered my phone was still off. Everyone must be worried sick about me.

Dad looked so relieved. His chest swelled and deflated, as if he had been crying and was now trying to regain control of himself. He lifted his arms as if to embrace me. But I backed away.

"Carly?" he asked, bewildered.

Thoughts still tumbled around in my mind, like balls in a Bingo machine.

"I thought you were—" I started to say.

"Who, Carly? Who?"

"*Him*. He was here. I saw him!"

"He's not real," said Dad. "He's never been real."

What was he saying? Did my dad think I was crazy? Was he playing games with me? But how could he possibly know about Raisin Face? I hadn't told him anything since coming to Reu.

"Miguel," I said, water dripping from my shivering lips. "He told you."

"No," my father replied, shaking his head. "You and I—we've been through this before, Carly. I had hoped by bringing you here—that maybe you'd forget."

"Forget? What are you talking about?"

Dad took a step closer to me. He looked so sad. "She's gone, Carly. Mom is dead."

Hearing those words felt like a spear through my heart.

"I know that!" I cried.

Why was he telling me this? What was he trying to do? I wanted to hit him, wanted to shut him up. I already knew my mother was dead. Why did he keep reminding me?

Dad ran his hands through his wet hair. "It was an accident. You've got to stop blaming yourself."

"Blame *myself*?" I was shouting. I wanted Dad to go away. I wanted him to shut his mouth! "Why would I blame myself? I don't understand!"

Dad was crying now. I couldn't see his tears through the rain, but I could hear it in his voice. My father's legs buckled and he dropped to his knees on the street. "I can't do this anymore," he said. "I can't watch you go through this again."

201

Go through this *again*? What was he talking about?

My dad's shoulders shook as his sobs mingled with the sound of the rain. A thought came to me. He had refused to communicate with his family once he'd met my mother, had waited until she was dead before he reached out to them, before he tried to mend his broken family ties. And now that she was gone, he wanted me to forget her altogether. It was horrible.

"You're ashamed of her," I said, the words sickening me.

Dad raised his fists to his temples and shook his head again, like he was fighting against something I couldn't see.

"No, Carly. Don't you see? I wasn't ashamed of your mother." Dad choked out the words. "How could I be ashamed of the one person who meant so much to me? If I was ashamed of anything, it was of myself, of what I was before I met her, of *this*!" He threw out his arms, gesturing all around him. "I didn't want you or your mother to know about my past, that I was the son of a poor, uneducated farm hand. I was young and stupid. As the years went on, I realized what an idiot I'd been, but too many years had passed. I thought it was too late to change things."

"I still don't understand. Why did you come back here?" I asked, trying to make sense of what he was saying. "Why drag me all the way to Reu? Why try so hard to make me forget her? It doesn't make sense!"

My dad wiped the rain from his face. "You've had a tough year," he said. "I know about the dreams, Carly. You've been having them since the beginning. At first, I wanted to tell you the truth about where they came from, what they meant, but the doctors said it would be too traumatic, that it would be best to let you forget. I brought you here hoping the past would finally be laid to rest."

"But that man," I said, desperate now. "I know him! I've seen him before!"

Dad raised his eyes to me, pleading to be understood. I remembered that look. He wore it at Mom's funeral as the preacher prayed over her grave. Dad was beside himself with grief. I was too drugged up with pain medication to feel much of anything. Someone had to take him away, had to help him into the car. And as the guests disappeared one by one, only I remained, shivering by myself in my wheelchair. In a few minutes, a nurse would come for me and take me back to the hospital. I don't remember much of the service. I just remember feeling numb and empty. I felt alone.

But I wasn't alone.

His was the sort of face you couldn't forget.

The memory came to me like vision, like a sudden ray of sunlight breaking through a storm cloud.

At the cemetery he had stood a short distance from me, an older Hispanic man dressed in gray coveralls holding a plastic trash bag. His face was dark and deeply lined with scars. The texture of his skin reminded me of a raisin.

I had watched him as he bent over and picked up a wilted bouquet of roses from a grave and dropped it into his bag. Then he moved on to another grave and picked up another dead bouquet. After a while, he stopped and turned toward me. He looked at my mother's coffin, and then he looked at me. There was a profound sadness in his eyes, and I knew that he understood.

He had made no attempt to communicate, but his eyes said more than words ever could. He had experienced a loss himself—a child, his mother, his wife? I'd never know for certain. But in that moment when our eyes connected, I understood the grief we shared. Then he went back to clearing the graves of the dead flowers, our connection severed. But still, I watched him. As he moved from grave to grave, petals escaped from his bag. The breeze lifted them, weightless for a moment, before they fell to the ground where they were left behind, scattered across the snow.

Petals in the snow.

Suddenly, my mind jerked out of this memory and skipped backward, flipping through lost days like pages on a desk calendar. The pages stopped on Christmas Eve one year ago.

The dreams. The past.

It all came rushing back.

Thirty-Four

IN SIXTY SECONDS, MY MOM WILL BE DEAD.

We are driving down Telegraph Highway, our headlights cutting through the inky blackness.

Snow is falling.

The keys sway in the ignition, off beat with "Rudolph the Red-nosed Reindeer." Moms switches off the radio. The box in her lap is wrapped in red foil paper. The store didn't do a very good job. The white bow on top is lopsided.

Mom stabs the bow with her forefinger. "I told him to hurry, but maybe I should have wrapped it myself."

I clench the steering wheel, trying to keep the tires straight on the slick icy road.

"Careful," says Mom. "Why don't you pull over and let me drive?"

But I'm too angry to respond. The clock on the dash says it's a quarter past seven. John would have come to the house already, come and gone because I wasn't there. Mom insisted on getting a last-minute gift, a gift no one needs.

"I was supposed to be home by now," I say, intentionally irritated.

"I'm sorry," Mom says. "But I had to get it wrapped."

"We didn't have to come. Dad has enough gifts already."

Mom clenches her jaw. "It isn't for Dad."

Not for Dad? Then why the hell did we come at all?

The front tire hits a patch of ice.

"Slow down!" Mom shouts.

"I am!" My irritation has turned to anger. "If I go any slower, we won't be home until midnight!"

"Carly — "

"John probably thinks I stood him up on purpose!"

The tires hit another patch of ice. The car hydroplanes. Mom grabs the steering wheel, but the car veers violently to the left.

Then I see the lights up ahead — in our lane.

No.

I realize too late — we are in the wrong lane.

The muscles in my arms seize up as I yank the wheel to the right, but the car will not obey.

It happens so fast —

The sounds of metal and glass popping, exploding —

The car spinning, throwing me against the door —

Pain erupting in my leg —

Someone screams, and I realize that it's my voice I hear.

Then it's over.

I don't know how much time passes before I open my eyes. At first, I just see flurries of snowflakes falling above me, white against the black canvas sky. I am not in the car anymore. I am lying in the snow.

I turn my head, feel the frigid ice against my cheek. I see our car, its front bumper fused to a power pole, the hood collapsed like an accordion. I see red spots all around, rose petals on a carpet of white.

Where did all these flowers come from?

I blink hard. Then suddenly, everything is red – red lights spilling blood over the world. Flashing – on, off, on, off – glinting off the wrecked car. Sparkling on the snow.

I hear sirens, and then I understand...

There are no roses here.

"My God. I was driving."

The realization drives hard into my brain, sending shockwaves through me.

My dad reaches for me, grabs hold of my shoulders. "Carly, don't," he urges. "It's better to forget."

"If I hadn't gone with her that night – "

"She would have gone anyway."

But I wasn't listening. Dad's voice was nothing but a meaningless echo. I look down into his imploring eyes.

"I killed her," I said.

The anger I felt before was gone, replaced by a terrible ache in the center of my soul. I felt my dad's fingers pressing into my shoulders, his warmth and concern burrowing into my flesh.

"I wanted you to forget," he said, still crying.

I never saw my mother dead. I only saw the petals of blood in the snow, and later, her coffin. Maybe my brain couldn't wrap itself around the idea that she was gone, not if I hadn't seen her for myself. So how could I deal with the fact that I — ?

I killed my mother.

If it is possible for a heart to stop beating and still live, mine did. In the days after the accident, I had felt it slowing, its rhythm decelerating like a music box winding down to its final notes. When it stopped completely, and that hollow space inside me formed, I somehow kept breathing and moving and eating and sleeping.

I kept dreaming.

Now those dreams had surfaced, like a long submerged sunken ship rising and breaching the surface of a stormy sea. I felt the pressure of an entire ocean behind my eyes, and my hollow place shattered into a million fragments, the shards erupting out of me in messy sobs.

My father was still kneeling there in the street, the water rushing around him like a stone in a river. I dropped to my knees in front of him, facing him. He slid his arms across my back and gathered me into them. And we knelt there together, crying in the rain, our lines of distinction blurring.

Thirty-Five

I AWOKE ON MY BED FULLY CLOTHED. My shoes and socks had been removed and lay in the corner of the room. Through the window, the moon was visible and the sky had not yet begun to grow light. I vaguely recalled stumbling home with Dad in the dark. Abuela had helped me into bed, but I was exhausted and must have fallen asleep before my head hit the pillow.

I glanced at the clock. It was nearly five am.

I lay there for a very long time. I felt numb. My head throbbed, and I wanted water. After a while, I dropped my feet to the floor and stood up. I reached for my art box and then opened the bedroom door.

A strange light emanated from the garden. I walked toward it, a lump forming in my throat. The lemon tree had been decorated with silver tinsel. Colored lights blinked rhythmically from its branches, illuminating the garden and veranda in a glow of red, green, blue, and gold. Several brightly wrapped packages lay at the tree's base.

It was unlike any Christmas tree I had ever seen, but it was beautiful just the same. I tilted my head back and looked up at the moon. The storm had broken, and the stars twinkled in the vast cobalt sky. Never had any night appeared more serene. It seemed horribly wrong, as if the world itself were mocking my grief. It wasn't just that my mother had been gone now for an entire year, but that she was gone because of me. How could anyone understand how I felt? How could I expect them to?

No one else was awake yet, so I decided to go for a walk. This time, though, I decided it was best not to freak everyone out. So, I tore a sheet from my sketch pad and left a note on the table for my dad, telling him where I planned to go and that I'd be back in time for breakfast.

The church was empty and silent when I opened the door and slipped inside. I wondered if the doors would normally be locked this time of morning, but since last night was Christmas Eve and today was Christmas, I suspected the doors were left open for people to come and go as they wished. There would probably be a special mass a little later in the morning. I wouldn't stick around that long. I just wanted a few minutes alone to think.

I slid into a pew and took in the room. Nearly every candle, several dozen at least, was lit, their flames gently shifting in their glass containers. Their combined light illuminated the chapel in a soft glow and cast pale luminescent circles across the images of Christ. Sitting here surrounded by God and his apostles felt somehow holy.

I set my art box beside me on the pew. Then I slid forward until I was on my knees, my hands clasped on the back of the pew in front of me. I had never been a praying person. I didn't even pray when I found out my mother had died. I hadn't known I could. I suppose part of the reason was that my parents were not religious people and never taught me how. I couldn't even say now that I had a clue what to do. But being there in that place, knowing what I now knew, I felt compelled to try.

"God," I began uncertainly. "Jesus." His name fell from my lips in a whisper.

"It's my mother, see. She left me — passed away — a year ago. And I — "

My eyes lifted to the statue of Mary holding the baby Jesus.

"I miss her."

I lowered my face and rested my forehead on my hands. Inside, I felt so much emotion: sadness, regret, longing. It had been so long since I'd felt anything, it was almost too much to bear.

"I know it was an accident," I continued. "And I know my dad says it wasn't really my fault and that I shouldn't blame myself, but I do. So, I want to — I *need* to — tell you I'm sorry."

My voice fell silent. I knelt there for a few minutes saying nothing. Perhaps I was waiting for an answer, for

God to open the heavens and tell me everything would be okay. But that didn't happen. Instead, I heard the creak of the chapel door opening behind me. I quickly got up off the floor and scooted back into the pew. I kept my hands clasped, though, and laid them in my lap. Was it time for mass? Would more people be coming in soon? Maybe it was time for me to leave.

I stood up and stepped into the aisle.

"Going so soon?"

I looked up and saw Miguel standing in front of me.

"I was hoping I could join you for a while." He motioned to the pew. "Do you mind?"

We sat down together, and he reached for my hand, surrounding it with both of his.

"You okay?" he asked.

I started to tell him that I was fine, but that would have been a lie. And I was tired of lies. I shook my head.

"I see," he said. "I stopped by a few minutes ago to see how you were doing after last night. Your dad called Dora and explained everything."

I couldn't look at Miguel. I felt too ashamed. "So, you know what happened."

"About your mom? Yeah."

"And you know I did it. I was driving the car that night. My mom died because of me."

I expected him to act like my father, to beg me not to blame myself. To let it go. To forget. Instead, he squeezed my hand.

"That must be a heavy burden for you to carry," he said. "Is that why you're here?"

At last someone got it. I could never just forget. Even when my conscious memory blocked out the truth, it found ways of sneaking through, in my dreams and my sketches. I wanted to cry, but I had cried myself dry last night. But that didn't mean I didn't feel.

"I guess I'm here to ask forgiveness. But it's really not God's forgiveness I'm looking for."

I thought it would sound silly, but I didn't care. It was the truth. I told Miguel because he was the one person I thought would understand.

"What do you mean?" asked Miguel.

I hesitated. How could I explain?

"To start with," I began tentatively, "there was the man with the scarred face. He wasn't real after all. I mean, he *was* a real person, but I only saw him once, at my mother's funeral. My brain has been struggling to sort out so many memories, I guess I kept on seeing him, even when he wasn't there. I just couldn't face reality."

Miguel listened without interrupting.

"The night of the accident," I continued. "Mom asked me if I would come with her to the store. I didn't want to go. It was Christmas Eve and it was snowing out. I told you that much before. Well, the reason was that I was expecting someone. A guy from school."

Miguel listened patiently. I felt a little more confident, so I continued.

213

"I had liked this guy for a long time and he'd finally started to notice me. He was going to pick me up and take me out, not anything fancy. We were just going out for hot chocolate or something. Anyway, my mom asked me several times to go with her. She said she had to buy one last gift, but she hated going out at night alone. So, I went.

"I didn't have the best attitude, as you can imagine. And the whole trip took longer than it should have. When we left the store, I was already late for my date."

Behind Miguel and I, the chapel door opened again. Three more people came in. They walked reverently to the front pew and sat down. I spoke more quietly. Miguel kept listening.

"I was angry. I wanted to get home quickly, so I insisted on driving. But the roads were icy. We started arguing. The car swerved."

More people came in and took their seats. Several lit candles and prayed. I was sort of glad for the interruption. I wasn't sure how much more I could say before I fell apart again.

"Mass starts at six," said Miguel. His voice was tender.

"Is Abuela coming?" I asked.

Miguel shook his head. "No. She came last night. She's probably sleeping in, but I'll bet in an hour she'll be heating up tamales for breakfast."

"I guess we should go then."

Miguel grabbed my art box with his free hand and we stood to leave. But Miguel, still holding my hand, tugged me in the opposite direction. I followed him to the candles.

"Let's light one. For your mother," he said.

I selected a stick from the holder and held it to one of the lit candles. A new flame blossomed, and with it I lit another candle. I waved out the stick, and smoke curled up from the blackened wood.

We stepped back and watched the candles for a minute. The way they flickered in their individual glasses made them appear alive. I couldn't help but wonder if they did in fact touch the souls of the dead. I hoped they did. I hoped my candle would carry a message all the way to heaven.

The church was filling up now, so we made our way out of the building. Outside, the sky was just beginning to lighten. We took the steps slowly, my hand in Miguel's. When we reached street level we turned for home, but we weren't in any hurry.

"Did I ever tell you why my parents divorced?" Miguel asked after a while.

He hadn't told me, and I had never wanted to pry.

He continued. "Well, the real reason is my dad cheated on my mom. Not with Dora," he added hastily. "It was before that. I was around twelve, and my mom threw him out. I thought, once he'd gone that he would stay in touch, you know? But other than an occasional

215

phone call and a couple of birthday cards, I didn't hear from him for three years."

The sound of our steps echoed off the empty street. We weren't the only ones out this morning, but for the most part, Reu was only just waking up.

"My mom eventually remarried, and I got to be too much of a handful for her, I guess. So, she sent me to live with my dad. That was almost two years ago. By then, he was with Dora."

I loved feeling my hand in Miguel's. He was so full of life and energy. I hated to think how abandoned he must have felt, first with his dad leaving, then his mom.

"It must have been very painful," I said, though no words could really express what we both were feeling.

"It was. Still is." Miguel smiled at me, but I could see the hurt and anger brewing behind his eyes. "I thought my relationship with my dad would improve once I moved in with him, but he's gone as much as ever, traveling for business. And now it's not just me he's leaving behind. It's Dora too."

He let go of my hand, his fingers clenching into fists. "It pisses me off, you know?"

We stopped walking. Miguel pressed his eyelids closed and took a deep breath. When he opened his eyes to look at me, I could tell he was calmer.

"Anyway," he went on, "the reason I'm telling you this, Carly, is because you and me, we're the same. We both keep holding on tight to something we have no control over. My dad? He'll never change. I can either let my anger destroy me from the inside out, or I can forgive him and move on."

The morning was becoming steadily brighter. I could even feel the sun's warmth on my face. What Miguel said made sense, at least for him. But my situation was different.

"I don't understand, Miguel," I told him. "Are you saying I should forgive my mother for leaving me? She didn't do anything wrong."

"No, that's not what I'm saying at all, Carly." Miguel set my art box on the ground and took both my hands in his. He gazed meaningfully into my eyes. "You need to forgive yourself."

Forgive myself. How could I ever do that? I pulled my hands away from him and started walking. I wrapped my arms around myself. I thought Miguel had understood me, but now I wasn't so sure.

He caught up to me and took my arm.

"Hold up," he said. "Did I say something wrong?"

I stopped and turned to face him, but the tears had started, falling as hard as they ever had.

"I told you before I asked God for forgiveness." I tried to keep my voice steady, but was failing miserably. Miguel pulled me close to him. I buried my face in his shoulder, my tears soaking into his shirt.

"But what I really need to know," I managed to say through my sobs, "is if my mother forgives me."

Thirty-Six

BY THE TIME WE REACHED ABUELA'S HOUSE, the sunrise was in full bloom. Not a trace of the storm remained, and Christmas couldn't have started with a more beautiful morning. Miguel and I had stood in the street holding each other until I finally got myself under control and my crying had subsided. We walked the rest of the way in silence, but it was a comfortable silence, a familiar silence.

Miguel saw me safely to the door but then explained that he needed to get back to Dora. They would come over a little later for breakfast. He kissed me goodbye, and I let myself into the house.

I went to the kitchen and filled a glass with water. The house was as still as when I'd left an hour earlier. So, I set my art box on the table, opened it, and removed the pad of paper. I was about to start sketching when a voice interrupted me.

"We missed Las Posadas." My dad stepped out from the living room. He must have been sitting there in the shadows, waiting for me to come home. "The whole family went from house to house last night looking for a place for Mary and Joseph to rest, but all the inns were full."

"Sounds exciting," I said. "I'm sorry you missed it. I'm sorry you had to spend your night looking for me."

Dad nodded toward the kitchen where a platter of tamales waited on the counter.

"Hungry?" he asked.

I sat down at the table and peeled away the banana leaf from a tamale. It looked like a square yellow pillow with dark treasures embedded inside. I took a bite.

"Mmmm," I purred as the savory flavor of the masa merged with the sweet prunes and raisins. "This is really, really good." I took another bite, then added, "You weren't kidding when you said I'd like tamales."

Dad helped himself to one and sat down with me at the table.

"So, how are you feeling?" he asked.

I took another bite of tamale and washed it down with a swig of water. "You mean, other than like there's a rock in my chest where my heart should be?" I replied. I didn't want another flood of tears. "I'd be lying if I said I was fine. But it's better this way, knowing the truth."

Dad nodded thoughtfully. "I couldn't bear to see you hurting so much. I thought I could make it all go away."

"It's okay, Dad. Really. I'll deal with it in my own way, in my own time. And it will be easier with your help. Now, what about you?"

Dad hesitated for a moment, and then gave me a reassuring smile. "I'll be fine," he said. "With your help."

We ate our tamales quietly, enjoying the silent house. After a while Dad asked, "What do you have there?"

I turned my sketchpad toward him so he could see. "I've been working on a farewell gift for Miguel." I waited for some look of disapproval, some critical comment, but none came. "It's not my best," I continued, "but it's good to be painting again."

"May I?" asked Dad. I handed the sketchpad to him and waited for his reaction. His eyes examined the page for several moments. Finally, he handed it back.

"You've captured the different shades of green perfectly," he said. "When you're finished with it, do you think you could make one just like it for me? I could use a portrait of my favorite tree."

I turned towards the garden. Except for the tinsel and the lights, I had to agree the likeness was exceptional.

"Who's Santa?" I asked, gesturing toward the tree. "I don't remember you packing any lights."

"I wish I could take the credit," said Dad. "But your mystery elf is Miguel. To inspire you, he said."

So, Miguel had decorated the tree. I wasn't surprised.

"Do I sense a hint of admiration in your voice?" I asked.

"He's not so bad," replied Dad. "He was the one who told me you'd left last night. He showed up with a box of firecrackers, and you were nowhere to be found. You know, it's not that I didn't like him. I was worried about you, that's all."

So, his disapproval hadn't been about Miguel. It had been about me. He knew what I was going through, that I was vulnerable. He didn't want anything to happen to me.

I reached for his hand and gave it a squeeze. "Thanks," I said.

Once we had finished our tamales and cleaned up the table, Dad stretched his arms and yawned. "It's after six o'clock," he said. "I guess it's officially Christmas. In Guatemala, we generally open presents on Christmas Eve, but since we were sort of occupied last night, how about we open ours now?"

He walked over to the tree and picked up a square package wrapped in red paper. My mother's gift from last Christmas Eve! The white bow was a bit crumpled and the paper damaged and patched in a couple of places.

"Where did this come from?" I asked, trying to keep my emotions in check. "I thought it was lost in the accident."

Dad smiled thoughtfully. "It got a little banged up."

I touched the plastic ribbon, running it between my thumb and forefinger. An envelope with my name was taped to the front.

"Mom made out the card before she left home that night," Dad explained. "She'd seen what she wanted in an ad and had to go get it."

"What is it?"

"Open it and find out."

I opened the envelope and withdrew a plain sheet of stationary. The handwriting on it was my mother's, and my eyes welled up with tears as I read the note:

> *December 24th*
> *Dearest Carly,*
> *I watched you while you slept last night. I can't believe how much you've grown. What happened to that funny little girl that used to color on the kitchen walls? You have been my one source of joy in this life.*
> *Always remember how much I love you, and that I will forever be your guardian angel.*
> *Merry Christmas.*
> *Mom*

"After everything that happened," said Dad softly, "I didn't think it would be right to give it to you. That it would be too...hard. So, I put it away for a while. Until last night, I still wasn't sure if you could handle it, but I know your mom would have wanted you to have it either way."

His voice cracked, and for a moment I thought he might cry, but he took a deep breath and pulled himself together.

Carefully, I removed the wrapping paper and opened the box. There, resting among sheets of neatly folded tissue paper was a delicate glass angel with a gold halo and wings.

My breath caught in my throat. The gift had been for me. We had gone to the store because Mom wanted to replace the angel I had broken, the one that had been plaguing my dreams ever since.

I gently lifted the angel out of the box. It was so intricate, every detail so fine. A work of art. Was this the sign I'd been hoping for? Did my mother forgive me?

I noticed that even though I had removed the angel, the box still had weight to it. I moved aside the tissue paper in the bottom and discovered one more gift—a mirror with a white ceramic handle and frame. Another note lay inside, written on the back of a business card from the store we'd visited the night she died:

> *Saw this in the store and had to buy it for you. You are so beautiful! If you ever doubt it, just look in this mirror.*

"*Es igualita a su mamá,*" said Dad, brushing a strand of hair out of my face. "Abuela told you that when we first arrived. Remember?"

I looked at my reflection. I had never seen the resemblance before, but now I saw my mother in the curve of my brow and the shape of my nose and lips. I saw my father there too, his dark hair and eyes, his

223

narrow cheekbones. I placed the mirror back in its box and laid my mother's note and letter on top.

"This means more to me than you know," I said. "Thank you for letting me have them."

I set the box aside and reached into my sketch box. "I have something for you, too." I removed the leather bundle of brushes from the box and held it out to my father. He took it and fondly caressed the leather.

"All these years," I told him, "I remembered the touch of Mom's hand on mine, guiding my brush. But I was wrong. Mom didn't teach me how to paint. You did."

I reached over and laid my hand on top of his. He smiled at me, for real this time, and I smiled back.

"What about your angel?" Dad asked.

I looked at mother's gift in my hand. I knew where it belonged. I stood up and settled the angel on the topmost branch of Abuela's lemon tree.

"It's perfect," said Dad, nodding his approval.

And he was right. It was perfect.

Thirty-Seven

WE STAYED IN THE GARDEN for another hour, watching as the rays of morning light spilled across Abuela's garden like liquid gold. Abuela emerged from her room first and set immediately to warming up tamales. Soon Papa Beto settled into his favorite chair to read the paper.

It wasn't long before Dora and Miguel came over. Other members of the family dropped in as well, bringing tamales and wishing us *Feliz Navidad*. Knowing that we were leaving the next day, they kissed my father and me farewell and told us to come back again soon. Some of them, including Dora, cried. As the day wore on, I hoped Miguel and I might steal a moment alone, but it was a busy, wonderful day I would never forget.

As the day finally came to a close, I headed to my room to begin packing. It was hard to believe our trip to Guatemala was over. Tomorrow we would leave Reu before sunrise, drive to the capital city, and take a flight back to Los Angeles. A lot had happened since we'd arrived here, and I wondered if we would ever come back. I hoped so.

I emptied the dresser my clothes had inhabited during my stay in this room and laid them in my suitcase, then I followed that with my Quetzal jacket. I hadn't had much opportunity to wear it, as Reu was too warm, but back home it would be perfect. I touched the delicate woven bird on the back, the symbol of the Gods, of sacrifice. A slight shudder went through me as the memory of lying on that stone altar in Zaculeu returned. It swam around other images: the cemetery, Raisin Face, blood on the snow, but I closed my eyes and shook them out of my head. Dad said that what I'd experienced here in Reu—the dreams and seeing Raisin Face—had not been the first time, but I was determined that it would be the last. I wanted to keep my mind clear. I wanted to remember.

The last things to go in my suitcase were my mirror and the glass angel from my mother. I tucked them both carefully between the layers of clothes to help protect them. These treasures meant more to me than I could express. When I lost my hat that day at Champerico, I thought I had lost my one connection to my mom. The mirror and angel helped to restore that connection. They were also an answer to my prayer, the only prayer I had ever uttered in my life. I would never get over losing my mom, nor would I ever really forgive myself. But with my mom looking out for me, I would heal in time.

As I was zipping up my suitcase, there was a knock on my bedroom door. A moment later, a welcome face popped into view.

"Hi, Miguel," I said wistfully. This would be our final moment together, which made his appearance bitter sweet.

"Hey," he said. "Can I come in?"

"Sure. I was just packing."

I expected him to sit down on the bed or the chair, that we'd chat uncomfortably for a while, and then say our goodbyes. But instead, he strode across the room, curled his arms around me, and pressed his lips against mine. Though his boldness took me by surprise, it only took a second for me to respond, kissing him back with equal fervor.

When he finally pulled away, he looked at me with an intense gaze. "You're coming back. Someday, you're coming back."

"I will," I said. "I have good reason to now."

He smiled. "And now I have a good reason to visit California."

I finished zipping my luggage shut and set it on the floor. "Done," I said. "Would you mind carrying this to the car for me?"

He obliged. Dad was already outside, loading up Papa Beto's trunk with our things. Everyone except Dora had said their final farewells for the night and gone home. In just a few hours' time, after what promised to be a fitful night of sleep, we would be gone too.

Dad accepted my suitcase from Miguel, squeezed it in, and shut the trunk. He turned back and gave Miguel a stern look. For a moment, I thought he would say something rude, but instead he held out his hand.

"Thanks," he said, "for everything."

Miguel took his hand. A mischievous look passed between them.

"You ready?" Dad asked.

"Ready," said Miguel.

I glanced at Dora. The grin on her face indicated that she was in on this too.

"What's going on?" I asked.

Without answering, Miguel retrieved a paper bag from the back seat of Papa Beto's car. He held it up like a trophy.

Dad took the bag from Miguel. "Since Christmas Eve didn't turn out quite the way we had planned—"

"Missing Los Posadas, for example," Miguel added teasingly.

"We decided to celebrate in our own way." Dad opened the bag, reached in, and pulled out a long string of firecrackers. I was keenly aware that no one else in the neighborhood was lighting firecrackers at that moment. All that had occurred the night before.

"But Christmas is over," I said, "and it's late." Though I had to admit the idea of having our very own celebration right here in front of Abuela's house filled me with giddy anticipation.

Miguel wrapped an arm around my waist. To my relief, Dad didn't even blink.

"It's not over yet," said Miguel.

Dad rooted Abuela out of the kitchen and Papa Beto from the card table, and then we headed across the street to where the palm trees rustled in the night breeze. Dad held up the firecrackers.

"How about we wake up the neighborhood?"

"Dad, I can't believe you're doing this!" I said, laughing.

"Will you do the honors?"

He handed me a match. I struck it and held the flickering red flame to the wick. It sprang to life with a loud hiss. Dad tossed the string of firecrackers into the street, and the popping and screeching began.

In that single moment, I became keenly aware that life as I had known it would never, could never be the same. My mom was gone. Nothing could change that, but somehow standing here with my family, I felt more at home than I had in a long time.

Thank you for reading

Petals

We invite you to post a review on
Goodreads
& your favorite online book retailer.

For a free e-book, join our mailing list at:
www.SkyrocketPress.com

Acknowledgments

THIS BOOK HAS BEEN REWRITTEN SO MANY TIMES, I've lost track. I think I wrote the first draft back in 2005 or thereabouts. It was the first full-length book I ever wrote, and it was awful. Over the years and countless revisions, thankfully *Petals* developed into something entirely different than what I originally envisioned. There were many people who helped along the way, but quite frankly, I can't recall who most of them were. So, if you read an early draft of this book and are not mentioned here, please accept my sincerest apologies.

I do know that my daughter, Carissa, has played a huge role in shaping this book in more ways than one. Not only is she an amazing developmental editor with a keen eye for characterization and pacing, but she is also the inspiration for the protagonist, Carly. Like Carly, Carissa is of mixed heritage, half white (my side) and half Hispanic (her father's side). When she was eight years old, she accompanied her father on a trip to Guatemala, the same adventure I had undertaken a decade earlier. The country and culture made an astounding impression on us both.

Carissa has never had an issue with straddling two cultures. But in creating Carly, I wondered what might happen if she did? How would a teenage girl feel about being part of two worlds so vastly different from each other? These questions were fundamental in laying the foundation for *Petals*.

So, above all, I have to thank Carissa for letting me extract part of her to create a fictional character. (It's certainly not the only time I've taken such liberties.) The process is kind of like how God took a rib from Adam to form Eve. Carly was constructed of a small segment of my daughter. I hope the result is satisfactory.

I also have to thank my husband, Gonzalo Reyes, who was born and raised in Guatemala and who toted me along on a three-week journey there when we were engaged to be married, exposing me to one of the most beautiful places on earth. When I first began writing *Petals*, I wanted so much to preserve my impressions of his homeland, and a novel seemed the perfect vehicle. Also, he is a terrific editor.

I also borrowed parts of my husband's family members to construct other characters in the book, in particular, Gina and Chalo Reyes (my in-laws) and Patty & Juan Ramon Ramirez (my husband's aunt and uncle).

My parents, Ray and Cyndi White, were just as important in the creation of this book. Though they do not make an appearance in the story, they are always a source of inspiration for everything I write, as are my children: Carissa, Marcum, Stuart, Brennah, and Jarett.

I also need to mention Emma Michaels, Hayley Guertin, Gloria Treviño, Laura L. Hunter, Dorine White, and my amazing Street Team (Go Team!). And finally, thanks to all of you, my fans and readers. Without you, there would be no point to writing any story. You keep me motivated and inspired.

God bless you, and thank you!

About the Author

LAURISA WHITE REYES is the author of the 2016 Spark Award winning novel *THE STORYTELLERS*, as well as THE CELESTINE CHRONICLES and THE CRYSTAL KEEPER series. She lives in Southern California where she teaches English at College of the Canyons.

www.LaurisaWhiteReyes.com

Made in the USA
Lexington, KY
18 March 2017